THE
STARLIGHT LINE

THE
STARLIGHT LINE

BY
MATT MARSHALL

Red Giant Books

ISBN: 978-0-9905435-6-5

Printed in the United States of America.

www.redgiantbooks.com

Cover Illustration by Matt Marshall

Book Design by Ryan Walker

This book was completed with the generous support of the Community Partnership for Arts and Culture of Cuyahoga County, Ohio, through its Creative Workforce Fellowship program.

I

First and Last Chance

No one drives the locomotive,

No one tends the staring light,

Trains have never needed riders,

Trains belong to bitter night.

    —Thomas Pynchon, *Gravity's Rainbow*

IMMEDIATELY SHE WAS TALKING, BARELY WAITING FOR ME TO SLIDE MY ASS onto the barstool (before even able to order a beer or draw my wallet out even) lighting into me with talk of the place (which, as you'll see, was inextricably linked with herself, her own history—proved this was the only thing she had left) of Jack London and how he used to sit and write at that table over there (she slid off her stool at this point and walked over to the small table, solid in its 100 years or what, and pointed to some knickknacks on the wall—the place smothered by them, around the tables, on the ceiling, behind the bar—and drove on in her inebriated state on Jack on Oakland on the whalers on ships on the neighborhood and on how this was a locals' bar, filled with friends and if—drawing out now a pamphlet with the history of the saloon printed cheaply on folded yellow paper—if you care to know more here it is, you should read it and here on the back is a list of resource books you can find at your library or bookstore)—Are you a reader?

—Yes, of course. Well, I *was*, at least.

—Then you know these places and don't need a dried up old woman to tell you where to find ... but if you want to, you should really read up on this place. Have you ever read Jack London?

—Ah, maybe a story or two when I was in school, but I really can't say for sure.

—Oh, you should. He's very important to these parts. He used to sit at this table right here and write. And! (She pointed at me.) And—study! As a boy he used to study right here. You don't believe me.

—No, of course I do. What reason ...

—Well, you don't believe me, but he did. Right here. I think sometimes you can see the spots from his books worn into the wood.

Here she traced the grain with a finger. Then the flat of her palm. Stopped her hand's motion and left it there.

—Right here, she says.

I have my pint now. Leonard has filled it for me, let it settle, then topped it off. It is good, if not (as always) thick enough. I used to think that one day I might find that sublimely thick, mellow Guinness that would release all the world's mysteries. I humored myself with fantasies of such an elixir, laughing philosophical absurdities through the numerous pints that poured into my brain and sealed it in concrete. Such play, over years, finally wrecked any notion I had of obtaining enlightenment through drink. Still, I soldier on. The joy, after all, is in doing, not achieving, as they say.

Helen brings the yellow pamphlet over and shoves it in between the glass and my hand. She takes up her seat again two stools down from me closer to the door. She asks Leonard for a refill of her wine. He nods and takes the glass.

—Where you from then? she asks in a warm, friendly manner that later, upon reflection, seemed also to have something of an accusatory character about it.

—Cleveland, I admit.

—Cleveland?! And she's popped through the ceiling. Cleveland? Well, Jesus Christ, a Midwestern boy, like myself. Well (her fresh wine arrives and she takes it almost without looking, spinning back and forth on her stool, continuing to talk to me in her excitement) I'm a dried up old woman obviously—not a boy—but you know what I mean. Had a husband for 42 years till he croaked on me—from Kentucky—now I just sit around and talk to Midwestern strangers like yourself. No, you'd be surprised how many people from back that way wander in here.

I shrug.

—Where'd you hear about this place, anyway?

—In a tour guide.

—Ah, well, you gotta find it somehow, she decides, her mood seeming to turn as sour as mine for a measure or two, but then —Holy shit, Ohio, she muses with renewed vigor. Cleveland … Probably ten inches of snow on the ground there, huh?

—Got a decent storm just before I left, yeah.

—Yeah, wow, I remember that.*

—How long'd you live there?

—Oh, long time. Probably 12 years. Let's see. Yeah, 12, I think. (The wine spins slowly, heavily in her glass.) I'm drunk.

—You ready for another? It's Leonard talking to his friend on the other

---

* "I, who had never known girl's love, nor woman's love, nor the love of children; who had never played in the wide joy-fields of art, nor climbed the star-cool heights of philosophy, nor seen with my eyes more than a pin-point's surface of the gorgeous world; I decided that this was all, that I had seen all, lived all, been all, that was worth while, and that now was the time to cease." Jack London, *John Barleycorn*, pp. 70-71.

side of me. Both just-outta-college kids with nothing better than this on a Thursday night (well, Leonard working, obviously, but ...) hanging out talking and his friend, Ramón, takes another Anchor Steam, Mexican boy, or of Mexican descent anyway, an American clearly as he is clean clear talking English when he speaks and asks how I drink the Guinness and I tell him it's all there is to drink though he says it's too heavy and I say it's not heavy enough.

—Yeah, my husband used to sail. We'd stay out on the boat for weeks sometimes, then finally just decided to move in full time. It's docked right outside here. Used to be a lot of people'd do that and it'd be wild times up here at night and out on the boats, everybody partying. Rougher times, too. Not all the shellac and pink paving stones you see out here now. Authentic! But then the economy went boom and all the yuppies and tourists came flappin' over. And a couple of the old guard died, like my husband. Left me the boat and a lot of money in the bank, though, so I'm set till I kick it. Which is still a long time off, God willing.

She crosses herself.

The establishment's Chorus descends to the stage from the plethora of hats and helmets hanging from the ceiling, giving ghostly heads to the remnant lids of more spirited times, their raspy voices heavy and spitting like chugging locomotives.

CHORUS: When you gonna die? Yeah—*When? When?*

HELEN (her head tossing about to track the voices): Never. I ain't never gonna die. What's wrong with you?

CHORUS (along with me and Leonard and Ramón now): When?!

HELEN: Never, I said.

CHORUS: Everybody gotta die sometime. You do to!

HELEN: Nope, not me. Never. Screw you young, full-of-death fools. I believe in never.

CHORUS: Never! Raise a glass to Never!

The three of us at the bar drink, with Leonard the odd man out.

—I'll drink myself drunk into the grave, Helen says.

—Amen, sister.

—Amen to you.*

Leonard turns to switch CDs in the player on the shelf above the register.

—When'd you bring that thing in here? Ramón asks.

—Came from home. Dad got a new one, so …

—Yeah?

He chooses Radiohead. The first strains of "Airbag" coming over the small speakers on the shelf behind the bar (only now just seen amidst the knickknacks and pictures, foreign currency and such taped to the wall).

—But you guys need to know the history of this place! Helen implores. Really, you do. It's places like this that can't be lost and are being lost all the time cause people just don't give a damn. And it's a shame. A real shame. A damn shame.

Her head shakes vigorously. It's a common occurrence. Once her noggin popped off from a cause of her shakin' it, and it rolled around in wobbly circles on the floor.

—I need some more wine, Leonard.

Leonard pours it for her, laughing.

—My husband used to drink a lot of wine, but not anymore—he's dead. I drank a lot of wine with him, but for some reason it just ain't killed me yet. I'm leaving that to the damn cigarettes, which (she spins halfway round on her stool and looks out the open doorway to the just now beginning to darken evening) which now they won't even let me kill myself with here in the comfort

---

* 'Twas in Benicia, that, in the waters of the Carquinez Strait, where John Barleycorn had twisted young Jack London into thinking it was time to cease, nearly laying him low through the workings of Jack's own romantic imagination and thereby "drug-dream dragging [him] to death." *Barleycorn*, p. 71.

of a chair, but gotta parade out into the elements and stand up and smoke 'em. All the exercise from that—I *am* gonna live forever.*

She completes the spin now, coming all the way around till she's back again facing me.

—You ever been married? she challenges suddenly.

—No. No, I haven't.

—How old are you?

—35.

—Oh, okay, I see, you're gay. She says it flatly, with no intended malice or judgment, but simply as a matter of computational fact. Then her stool's on the move again, spinning her clumsily to heels clacking cross the warped and deeply slanted wood floor (in fact, if not for the 1906 earthquake disrupting the earth beneath this shack of a bar and lifting its front end—or lowering its back, depending on how you want to look at it—Helen might well've had her shins tossed up against the two-by-six plank dropping down from the door and out face first onto the modern bricks of Jack London Square) but she negotiates the terrain safely somehow and is now out walking away from the building, her lighter struck, flame reaching toward the cigarette jutting starboard on her lip.

—She's always gone, Leonard tells Ramón now.

—She is every time I come in here.

—She mentions her husband one more time, I'm gonna go dig him up

---

* After Jack London died, his daughter, Joan, wrote a book about him. Fat chance a daughter of mine would do that, even if I had one. *Jack London and His Times*, she called it. Did I read it even? Only thing I really remember about it (and why this, I have no idea) was that she sent a copy down to Leon Trotsky when he was exiled in Mexico. Apparently the old Bolshevik had helped her with the book somewhat. He also supposedly called London's *The Iron Hand* a work of genius for foreseeing way back in 1907 that fascism would be the direct result of a crushed proletariat, or something like that. I think Joan sent Trotsky his copy of *The Iron Hand* too.

and kill him again.

—He's probably still lying in state on the boat, Ramón observes.

The two of us (Ramón and I) drink. Leonard spits into a cup with water his tobacco juice.*

—How long has he been dead? I ask.

—God knows. Two or three years, I think.

—You know him?

—No.

—I've heard stories about him.

—Yeah, me too.

—Crazy fuck.

—She was fine, I think, till he keeled over. Drunk every night now. Don had to call Howard again last night to come in and carry her outta here. She was going on and on about something—yelling basically—then stood right over there and almost peed on the floor. Sad.

—Right there?!

—Yeah.

—What the hell was she doing?

Leonard shrugs. He spits into his cup.

—Sad.

—That's hilarious.

—And she's like that every night? I ask.

—Yeah, pretty much.

—I wish I'da seen that, Ramón chimes. Her just standing there peeing away.

---

* Then, on a night in late November, he succumbed. His body poisoned more from years of uremia than from the heavy dose of morphine supped from the now empty bottle discarded on the floor by his bed. Though, to be sure, he had mused on suicide throughout his years.

—Sad.*

—I pissed in a bar once.

—Where the hell was that?

—I don't remember the name of the place. Some place out a little ways from San José State.

—Who you with?

—Rich, those guys. I started to pull it out and Rich basically has to come over and tackle me.

—But you started?

—There was a bit of a puddle after we got off the floor, yeah.

—They boot your ass?

—Nah, that place? They didn't even know anything had happened. Rich said later one of the bartenders was bitching at us for spilling beer in the spot. That place was a hole.

—I don't know it.

—Yeah, I can't remember the name of it.

—Back with empty glass! Helen projects, the acrid scent of smoke pulsating from her throat.

—Hear! Hear!

Leonard carries the empty glass smudged of fingerprints and what over to the wine bottle now in other hand and with a tip of that said hand

---

* "It is impossible to move forward while leaving the woman far in the rear. Woman is the mother of the nation. From the enslavement of women grow prejudices and superstitions which shroud the children of the new generation and penetrate deeply into all the pores of the national consciousness. The best and most profound path of struggle against the superstition of religion is the path of all-sided concern for the mother. She must be raised up and enlightened. Freeing the mother means cutting the last umbilical cord linking the people with the dark and superstitious past." Leon Trotsky, "To Build Socialism Means To Emancipate Women and Protect Mothers," *Women & the Family*, p. 48.

commences the refilling, returns it now to proper owner, who begins in with it, now, forthwith.

—What you guys don't understand, and, no, I mean it—*Leonard!*— what you guys don't understand is that this place is very important and we need to save it.

—It ain't goin' anywhere, Helen. We're still right here. This place gets along fine.

—Yeah, now it does, yeah. Now it does. But after I'm down under, I don't know. I don't know.

Helen falls into contemplation (or some such) over her fresh glass of wine. Wind, or snoring, drifts in through the open door.

I take note of the clock in the lull. 7:32. A train I'm booked on leaves out at 9:47 from the Amtrak station two blocks down the road, where earlier in the day I dropped off my bags (including, with some trepidation, the messenger bag and its contents) before heading back into SF for a day of lounging, CD buying and the like, calculated to blow off steam, relax and forget, with pints now to take off the edge, before the necessary escape via train into the north. Leonard starts me another Guinness without asking and my head warms that extra bit, releasing a smile. The *inness* of it. I slouch in renewed confidence. Everything will be just fine now. It was foolish of me to worry. After all, none of it really matters. The risk has all been in my head. (And the reward too, most likely.) In the end the authorities aren't all that interested in checking the papers and belongings of every passerby, every traveler going here or there. This ain't the movies or the nightly news. The reality is that most questionable or truly illicit cargo passes through without a hitch. So don't worry. And even if that complex jumble I'm lugging around were to be drawn out and laid on the table for public perusal, what of it? Sure, there'd be a decent amount of tongue wagging and head shaking, fact chewing and breath bating for a while, but it would all die away fairly quickly and then pour into the next big revelation. No one really cares. In fact, they laugh at you for caring. Let it go. Drink another. You did what? Wild fuck. Hah—that's priceless! Here, drive this up your nose. Take this up your ass. Nobody cares. O what a story! Who was that again? Ah, it doesn't matter. That's *too* good. Let me buy you a round. Have another. Though there is, of course, the risk from those in the trade, if you really fuck up or expose the wrong people or cross their path at a particularly inopportune time or with a manner that conveys some kind of disrespect. Then there's no imagination too wild to contain what might be visited upon you. Look at that poor devil in Juárez who had his face ripped off and stitched into a soccer ball. But, again, that's the extreme. By and large nothing happens, and nobody cares. So write and reveal whom- or whatever you want. In the end, poor listless romantic, something other than a disgruntled subject of your pen will do you in. You'll be expunged not by the gun or the pickax, as might be your wont, but by the critic's scoff, the publisher's skittishness and the reader's indifference or forgetfulness. That's the death from writing, from trying to say a little something while you might. Condemned to tap out strident diatribes at the corner of the blogosphere while blubbering spittle into the hair of an unshaven chin. That's the glorious end for the writer's quixotic toil. That's how you'll be appreciated. Nobody cares. So wait here. What of it? The most you'll get is more drunk than you should.* Nothing but two more easy hours of drinking and lounging before trekking dark oceanside streets in the March perfect coolness to catch old train north overnight into Portland (of the further drinks then in observation car with that green Sinatra aching his "Where Are You?" question over headphones with soaring strings, through the restless night in train seat with the tubercular

---

* "I abandoned myself to the life, and developed the misconception that the secret of John Barleycorn lay in going on mad drunks, rising through the successive stages that only an iron constitution could endure to final stupefaction and swinish unconsciousness." London, *John Barleycorn*, p. 68.

gentleman next to me coughing apart his ravaged lungs, to hangover next day and kids screeching up the aisles the song of sad, overworked, overextended families on vacation with Café Tacvba this time in my ears, arriving to head straight to the bar in hotel to recover with needed pints—all my luggage lost (all but the messenger bag, that is, which I will keep tight to my person with all due, laughable diligence; the messenger bag that will, no doubt, prove to be the most expendable of all my possessions—better to have retained my socks!) yes, all of it traveling on to vacant parts unknown). But that would be later. And at present it remains still a fiction and might, theoretically, become nothing more than that. So for now just cool in the pour without notice—the beginning—the filling. There is nothing else.

—On business then? Helen asks.

—No, no. Vacation.

—Ah, vacation. I used to take a lot of vacations. Spent a summer in Alaska once nearly out in the wild. Beautiful country—beautiful. How long you staying?

—Taking the train out tonight. To Portland.

—Ah, the Starlight Line, right? Think that's what they call it.

—Don't know.

—Yeah, think so. Yeah … that's one thing I've always meant to do. Haven't gotten around to it yet, though. Haven't even been to Portland, if you can believe that. Tried to get some of my girlfriends interested a while back, but no dice. Someday, though. Yeah, that's something for years I've said I wanted to try—ride the Starlight Line.

The train chugs off into the depths of her glistening eyes.

—Well, that'll be cool.

—Hopefully.

—Sure. It's always good to get away. Train travels right along the shoreline there, right? Through the sequoias, by the mountains …

—Yeah, I think so.

—One of these days I'm gonna do that. You've convinced me. One of these days before I leave here. Or before I die.*

—You moving back to Cleveland?

—No, no. God, no. Have a good friend in Florida, so that's probably the way I'm headed. Once I sell the boat.

—Yeah, okay, Florida, I grumble. You can have it.†

—Ah, it's not such a bad place.

—It's all right, I guess.

—I like it.‡

—It's okay, but I'd never want to live there, right? One of those places.

—Well you're young, she says, waving it off. That makes a difference.

An Earlier Tale in Which Helen Takes a Boy (Her First)
I skipped the blue skies young tripped in grass and fell like you on knee on lollipop dirty so you never wanted ta suck it no more and what that's the way it is and goes and can't be helped and's quite nice once you get over the hump giving up striped dresses for

---

* Trotsky, who was dealt his fatal blow in the study of his fortified home (what today the media might refer to as a compound) on Avenida Viena in Coyoacán, Mexico City. His assailant a Soviet NKVD operative by the name of Ramón Mercader, aka Jacques Mornard, aka Frank Jacson, who had spent the preceding months posing as a friend and aid. "I don't want them to undress me," Trotsky told his wife, Natalia, before they wheeled him into the operation room. "I want you to do it." He never spoke to her again.

† The assailant let in to the study to discuss an article of his that defended the Soviet alliance with Nazi Germany in the early going of World War II, a position with which Trotsky agreed. Nevertheless, just before his death Trotsky would refer to Jacson's article—dismissively, it would seem—as but one dealing with French statistics.

‡ The assailant let in even though he looked haggard, wore a hat and carried a raincoat over his left arm on that sunny August afternoon.

plaids in short short way too shor Mommy yelling at me in the finger waggle and Pop it happens to the finest of us and to those in glasses and chopped off haircuts too even much quicker for this last set most times which goes against the grains of what we're meant to understand and take as truth on TV and where else those most physically favored often those most shunned or shied away from and Timmy with his sucked in cheeks and sneakers flopping over themselves was perfect for the picking unscared of him in T-shirts and straggly hair the few whiskers he shaved over and over again into razors that I wondered should it really cut like this but displaced pain somewhat I guess from what I heard later from others I squeezed the poor life out of him poor unsuspecting Timmy barely speaking a word to me the whole time that I loved him for it really and maybe more later realizing what a fragile creature he was wrung dry like some unwanted kitten in from the rain that night I clutched his hand a bit high on Coca-Cola and cigarette smoke drifting over from older students and parents and pulled him along through the or rather held him in such a way with my elbow stiff and pushed out that he had to lead me through the swirling throng leaving football night the chill you get but then and never more after that it must be only in the noses of the young to sense or else the universe really has been changing since it spilled into the '60s and now the air's so swirled and mixed up an autumn chill is not as it was before or was only in the mind ever and not a pure matter of physical olfactory suddenly alone then the two of us and I was certainly leading him this time never seemed so sure or at home with anything in my life his shirtless body quivering from chill or what and I touched him again laughing and he stayed stiff as a tree through the whole of it that I laughed and he laughed shakingly to copy me I think and I held him lying over top of him warm in the cold and held him and felt his throat flutter in my ear squeezing as if the last precious life outov 'im.

—So it's different. You should wait to go to Florida. But I'm due. I want my Bloody Marys in the sun.

—*That* I could handle.

—So tell me you're going to meet a girl up there in Portland.

—Who knows who I'll meet.*

—Come on, really?

—No, it'll be good, I lied. I lived with a girl not too long back. It was one hundred percent awful.

—Oh, come on.

—Terrible, I say, slicing the air with my hand.†

—She just wasn't the one.

Leonard finally remembers my Guinness, tops it off and brings it over to me. Goes back and marks another notch on my tab. I scan the paraphernalia behind the bar for a Discover symbol. Helen lifts the swirling wine to her open mouth and drains the glass. She waves it by stem at Leonard, her eyes two slits, grinning condescending granny face.

—So what happened to her? she asks turning back to me, once Leonard has with reproaching maturegrandchildlook (to the delight of Ramón) retrieved her glass and she's darted her tongue out once at him, she asks, What's the story?

—Later, maybe.

—Oh, come on now, none of this bullshit. Old Helen pours her heart out to you—I'd tell you about every wrinkle on my whole saddlebag body if you wanted me to—and here you go clam up.

---

* "I suggest calling the aim which is at the basis of both sadism and masochism: *symbiosis*. Symbiosis, in this psychological sense, means the union of one individual self with another self (or any other power outside of the own self) in such a way as to make each lose the integrity of its own self and to make them completely dependent on each other." Erich Fromm, *Escape From Freedom*, p. 180.

† After receiving the cranial blow from Jacson's pickax, Trotsky lingered for 25 hours and 35 minutes before dying at the Hospital de la Cruz Verde de México at 7:25 p.m. on August 21, 1940.

—It's really not that good a story.

—Who said it's gotta be good? Just tell it. I'm listening.

I shake my head at her.

—I got nothing, I tell her.

—Oh.

—That's the long and the short of it. Used to be I could spin out a tale on demand. Now, it hardly seems worth it.

—Which reminds me, she growls, jutting a nicotine-stained fingertip in my direction.* I was thinking about this just now when I went out for a smoke—what could you have possibly meant when you said you *used* to be a reader?

—When did I say that?

—When you first sauntered in here. I asked if you were a reader and you said *was*.

—Ah, okay, I laugh, yes. Something of a dodge, maybe. I still read, though I've cut down on it quite a bit. Just as I've all but quit writing.

—Oh, I see, so now you're a reader and a writer too? A real scholar, eh?

—I was, yes. A writer, that is.

—Hmph. Yes, of course, you *were*.

I try to squeeze back into her good graces, into her realm of familiarity.

—Hey, you know as well as I do, that where I come from, art isn't accepted as real work. So it's hardly worth sweating too much over it.

—But it's that way everywhere, she protests. That's no excuse. And remember, I hail from the George Szell era. I can't believe the Cleveland art culture has fallen off that much since then.

I shrug.

---

* "Little did I dream the fateful part Jackson's arm was to play in my life." Avis Everhard in Jack London's *The Iron Heel*, p. 32.

—Maybe not.

—Yeah, maybe not, she drones mockingly.

—Actually, I was a journalist for a time.* But I got tired of spitting out all the retreaded nonsense everyone expects to read. I was angry and thought I had unique, forceful things to say. So I quit and charged headlong into fiction. But, as it turns out, without nonsense, I really had nothing to say at all.

—Well, yes. Nonsense *is* where it's at, she acknowledges, falling into quiet consideration.

But the quiet is soon enough scattered by the leafy swirl of voices blowing in through the door, laughing now in their approach—shouts and playful sounds of one chasing another—and then a strange, sudden spell of silence before a burst of voices again and into the bar files a group of six or seven mostly young professionals followed by one tall, mustachioed man probably in his mid-fifties, his skin cured by the sun, oil pressing his thick hair up and back—a somewhat less severe copy of Carlos Fuentes, with a glassy cheerfulness where you might expect to find the author's penetrating gaze. He arrives at the bar, large bill out and at the ready in great hand of yellowed marble, thick wedding band on third finger pulling heel of hand to bar with its weight as he calls back to the rest of his group (now commandeering corner table) to collect their orders. After some back and forth (and the rehearsed chiding of one guy's request for white wine) he turns to Leonard and lays forth the order, lifting then dropping his hand so as to bounce bill from his fingers in high, dramatic fashion.

—Gotta reward the troops! he calls to Ramón, though the boy is close enough to be clapped upon the back (which he is). The wide grin spreads the man's mustache into two darkly oiled wings over his thin upper lip.

—I guess, Ramón grants him, a response that causes the dark wings to

---

* "Having burned my one ship, I plunged into writing." London, *John Barleycorn*, p. 147.

slowly close ranks around the fabulous monuments to Western orthodontia that were, but moments earlier, given full show by the executive's Fuentesian grin.* He remains bent over slightly to the bar, his arm still outstretched, fingers stuck in the position of having but moments earlier played a winning card. He straightens when the drinks arrive, life sparking within him again and laughing as he struggles to gather up his bounty.

—Never gonna make it, Ramón assesses.

—You ain't lyin', the man chortles. He turns and calls to the table for assistance. Two women come over and cart off two drinks each, garnering great howls of thanks from their comrades at the table.

—Met their sales goals this quarter, the man imparts to Ramón. Gotta pay the piper.

—Yes, I imagine you do.

—I gotta make the goals higher next quarter. This is getting too easy for them.

Ramón nods without smiling, and the man hoists the remaining drinks and takes them over to his team.[†]

Ode to Drink (or Drink Takes a Purpose)

Drinks requisition one upon the other to do their duty and die heartily for the cause to stack up to lift to rise to new glory and not worry about the tumbling later but always forward always on the Henry Miller the skins dried out by their advance

---

* "El presente de ayer, sin embargo, no era el pasado de hoy." Carlos Fuentes, *Los años con Laura Díaz*, p. 207.

[†] Six years after Trotsky's murder, Miguel Alemán was elected president of Mexico, profoundly changing the nation's course. Alemán allied the state with moneyed interests, rejecting and undoing many of the reforms Lázaro Cárdenas had enacted for the betterment of workers and peasants, and led the country into what would come to be known as the "Mexican Miracle"—a rush of unbridled capitalistic development that the new president professed would cause wealth to trickle down to the masses. *The Oxford History of Mexico*, pp. 575-76.

the victims that must fall then perhaps to the trenches of inertia not the drinks not the drinks themselves for they charge and are spent and expire leaving but the drying spit of their existence made from the start one and going one ringed like the liftings of a mushroom cloud inside a glass to give you notice of how you yourself might do it how you would if you could and the vanished drink mocks you popping bursts of laughter in your ear that in the 10 to 15 minutes it has exercised its potential more completely than you would ever in as many years—and you know it—the next in grip already at its height complete ready to play out its number which is one draining in the joy to sorrow and it's only in the continued gulping of these stories that you can perhaps in the end gain some small victory for yourself one tiny win which is nothing but your own satisfaction from exhaustion the having swallowed some for memory's sake to have done these things again and again so that it finally becomes something resembling a life even as it takes you over to the other side this victory the conspiring with the enemy against yourself.

—Howard? Helen. You up? Ha! Yes, yeah. Well, why not? Yeah, the same. Well whataya gonna do over there? No. Now. Now, Howard. Yes. Of course. Okay, good. Good. Sure, sure, I ain't goin' anywhere.

Her phone snaps shut. We await the pronouncement.

—Howard will be here presently!*

—Drinks for all! Leonard tosses his arms skyward, but then fails to follow through on his offer.

—Oh, Howard's good people.

—Howard's good.

—I love Howard, Ramón chimes.

—Howard, I say, lifting my glass.

—Here, Leonard announces, yanking two small bags of chips free from

---

* 8:12, if anyone's checking the clock.

their hooks on the wall and tossing them to us. Free chips to wait for Howard.

The minutes march on in a slow, steady advance, tilting to make increased headway through the jungle of boredom that ever renews its gaggle of heavy-hanging vines and confining underbrush, slashing their machete with refined precision on each cut so that their entry and passage into the night becomes more rapid and free, sallying forth, and forcing my mind in this moment to math. With but 45 minutes left before I need to pull myself free from this stool and head over to catch my train, I begin to plot the time in pints. If I figure one per 10 minutes, that means I can finish off four more (with just over a minute waver grace for each) before having to call it quits—still a good chunk of time on the drink clock. But is that advisable? Another four on top of the pond already swallowed could spill me over into stumbling, then a headache in the lag waiting for the train at the station (without chemical sustenance to spur me). So if I want to enjoy the ride a bit I should figure more cautiously. Fifteen minutes. That would give me three pints, on the nose, without too much rush, should keep things reasonable. And with the quarter glass still remaining in loose grip before me, probably the height of possibility without gulping. So then it is settled. The time has been accounted for, portioned off into neat 15-minute segments to accommodate three full drinks—one each to a block—to maintain with sufficient steam the body's need for oomph while not causing general breakdown and collapse nor a failing, if adhered to the plan as prescribed—not rushing forward one dose quick upon the last nor allowing one to spill over into the next's partitioned space, but keeping to the even keel and flow—for the gusto as it's called that will carry me over to the walk to the train and the waiting there in station for the engine's arrival till I am safe again within the confines of some manmade covering in a cozy seat, cold drink and munchies at the ready.

—Another? Leonard asks me.

—Please. And the plan has commenced.*

—So I heard you tell Helen you're out here on vacation? Leonard prompts when he brings my glass of medicine.

—Yeah. Spent a couple days here. Heading up to Portland tonight.

—Driving?

—No, no.

I take a drink from the glass he's just brought me, now that I'm cleared for it and his eyebrows are relaxing. —No, taking the train.†

—Ah. Keep at it then.

—Yes, sir, I will.

Ramón decides to pack it in. He raises himself on the rungs of the stool to reach over and clasp hands with his comrade and makes parting remark about calling on the morrow to perhaps arrange for some stellar activities, to which Leonard counters with reply that he'll again be working and could his friend possibly delay his call until the day after next, which reprieve Ramón grants him relaying his intention then to call upon the man promptly at four hours and twelve minutes after the striking of noon on the day following the

---

* Alemán continued to back Mexico's "Green Revolution," started during his predecessor Manuel Ávila Camacho's term in office. With funding from the Rockefeller Foundation and other U.S. philanthropies, crop production was greatly increased through the use of fertilizers, insecticides and hybrid seeds. Between 1950 and 1970 corn production grew by 250 percent, wheat rose from 300,000 to 2.6 million tons and beans nearly doubled. But while the modern production methods increased yields they also required less labor. Wages fell and hordes of unemployed rural laborers flocked to the cities or to the United States seeking work. "Hundreds of thousands of teenage women turned to domestic servitude or prostitution or, in some cases, something akin to a combination of both." *Oxford*, pp. 590-91.

† By 1957, with the aid of new paving equipment imported from the United States, Mexico had 15,000 miles of paved roads, including superhighways that stretched across the country and connected major cities. Trucks soon challenged the railroads in hauling freight. And the country was opened to what would soon become one of its greatest moneymakers: tourism. *Oxford*, pp. 585-86.

one which will dawn on us with the approaching unity of both hands long and short in their uppermost and with the calling at that prescribed hour they will settle upon their course, draw plans of action for the evening on maps if necessary, and execute with full force and conquer the objective of getting laid.

—Let it be so, Leonard says, releasing his grip from Ramón's and fashioning his free hand into a parting wave, which is returned in kind and ferries Ramón off through the open door and out skyward into the drifting night.

—So what is it you do with yourself back in Cleveland? Leonard asks after his friend has left and an adequate amount of time has been allowed to pass absent any speaking, time filled only with music (Coldplay now) and even Helen quiet and concentrating or vacant over her drink.

—Write. Or at least I did, as I was just telling Helen. So-called human interest pieces for newspapers, magazines, websites ...

—Not so hot?

—Awful. Endless. Just endless blather, really.

He laughs. —There's always this sense of the journalist's life being so intriguing.

—I can assure you, that's the furthest thing from the truth. At least in my case.

—Fired? he asks, laughing more freely.

—No. No, it was my choice. I choke up an uneasy laugh, betraying an inexplicable anxiety over his word "fired." No, I left it, I assure him. Had some thoughts of turning to fiction, but ...

—You know what you should try, Leonard begins, then scoots down the bar to take an order from a bubbly Asian chick (one who had earlier helped cart away drinks to the group in the corner) raising a holdonasec finger to me as he goes to help her then adds, There's a project I've heard of, while filling two beers for her, then going silent again splashing together the vodka-cranberry, collects the drinks and takes them to her, palms her money, changes it out in the cash register, turns but then stops and raises his hand with the dollar in it, acknowledging her wave to keep the remaining due her. He dumps it into his tip jar and begins wiping the bar with a damp rag.

—So what is this? I ask.

—Hm? Oh, yeah. Yeah. Something a friend of mine in school did—supposed to get the writing juices flowing. Write a novel in ...

—A month, I finish for him.

—Yeah, he pointing.

—Yeah, I've tried that. A co-worker suggested it a while back. Now I'm just trying to scrape together enough money to have him taken care of.

—That bad?

—No, it was all right. Forced you to write.*

—Didja finish?

I grin and take a drink of Guinness. I watch the clock. At the 14-minute mark I order my next beer, happy with my gauging and execution, the new pint arriving just seconds after 15 minutes have passed and the last of the first pint is being drained. I set the empty aside for Leonard and start in immediately on the second.

Laughter erupts from the corner table, and I turn just in time to see Fuentes arise from a grand, mock kiss, the Asian girl bent back over his right arm, laughing herself red in the face. The man releases her, then blows kisses around to the rest at the table, sits to a thunderous applause. Several drinks are raised. The Asian girl doubles herself over in laughter.

—High times indeed, Helen comments, not adverting her eyes from their fixed downward stare into her drink.

Leonard and I exchange grins, but refrain from passing verbal judgment on Helen's deflated state.

The next twenty minutes go by without incident: the corner table quiet

---

* "O I wish I could write!" Jack Kerouac, *Tristessa*, p. 86.

mostly, keeping their gathered mischief to themselves; Helen draped over her drink, oblivious seemingly to any movement around her (of which, as I've said, there is little); Leonard the only one to supply even the slightest bit of action as he fidgets with the CD player, selecting a certain disc, but then rarely allowing the first song to finish before heading back to the machine with a pained expression on his face to pick something else, hoping maybe, as I am, for that magical piece of music that'll spark the life in all of us, wash clean the soot that has settled on our brains and hearts and clear us to live only for the time being, sucking other shades in from the night to clutter about ourselves and surge chaos without consequences in our happy, gas-lit shack. But time is dimming and even my efforts are waning over final pint that I need to quaff the last third of it in a rush to stay the course—the tap of glass against mahogany (or whatever wood the bar might be made of) striking the bell on my round, and I present my Visa card to Leonard, settle up and hit the road.

I Take a Walk

Outside the air cool guides me by rail along the black somehow slick in not being wet streets head the whistle to night of coming things but still steady nice pleasant and not too drunk proving the maxim that if one lays plans and follows up whether be it in education in romance in business in charity in pure bacchanalia good things will pass upon him and he will not stumble nor feel dizzy but stay the course straight and reach his desired destination and people will say upon him that he is good and friendly and is a well-planning man who knows what's what and so forth and they will come upon him with questions and glorious offerings and he will not rebuke them nor look down upon them but will take them to his bosom saying unto them this and that and other such wisdoms sending them out then to do good and live by the light of his example to pass it around a bit to friends at dinner parties and they will and shall not forget him on holidays but gather family about themselves and roast animals to carve in his name and dip in gravy and swallow with wine in his remembrance this schedule-keeper and he will be happy of it and be damned if he ever lets the headache settle in on him and twist his brain to considering the many distractions in the world that might tempt him to stop pulling on his rope lifting that bail and the rest—he will catch his train and be off and be happy and well thought of and there the ending can descend on him nicely.

The train station was a brightly lit beacon, sitting off by itself in a hard field of modern bricks and steel garters, flags waving controlled welcome on poles out front, while the surrounding neighborhood of small shops, homes and factories sat by in dark repose, asleep, waiting. Inside it was cool and smelt faintly of cabbage or stale, soiled clothing. I waited in line behind a woman who kept weighing her departure-time options, asking and re-asking the attendant to give her the times, then repeating them back slowly as if numbers and time-telling were new to her. Finally she was asked to step aside while deciding, and only then seemed to notice my presence, frowning at my impertinence of having come along and positioned my body behind hers. But step aside she did, and I stepped forward and presented my ticket to the woman behind the counter.

—The train was late leaving out of Los Angeles, the woman relayed. Won't be here for another two and a half hours probably. We'll be checking people in around 11:30.

She handed the ticket back and I went over and sat in one of the blue fiberglass chairs in the lobby. I drew Pío Baroja's *El arbol de la ciencia* from my backpack and settled in to read. But only then did the cloud in my head present itself, causing the words on the page to become obscured in the paper's pulp, and the book's plot to trail off into space before refinding its track on roads I had rolled over several years earlier. After Christmas Eve dinner, and after deflecting all argument from his sister, the medical student Andrés Hurtado went to the train station and bought a third-class ticket to Valencia in order to inspect a house for rent in a nearby village that might serve his younger brother well in his recovery from tuberculosis. The night was cold and Hurtado awoke just before dawn nearly frozen through. A villager travelling in the train car with him offered the "delicate" young madrileño his blanket. Despite this insult to his physical character, Hurtado accepted the offer, and was happy to have the added warmth. As they travelled farther south, the landscape gradually changed, with hills and trees replacing the open flatland. La Mancha passed. Cerca de Játiva salió el sol. In Alcira, orange trees appeared, heavy with fruit, and the swollen Júcar river rolled by with a gentle current. El sol iba elevándose en el cielo. The Mercedes bus shifted gears and continued rolling across the sun-fired plains. An hour and a half outside of Guanajuato we stopped at a nondescript bus station and a handful of passengers dislodged. La Naturaleza y la gente eran otras.

I decided to give up the reading long before actually closing the book, using it instead as a shield that'd give object to my sitting—save me from being seen as too careless or stupid to have brought something along to occupy my time if not sleeping. But, in truth, I was watching the faces and bodies and clothing and luggage of the other passengers, trying to chisel from the collection of these items each person's story. What had brought them to that station at that particular moment in history and what, if anything, did the intersection of our lives at that time and place mean?

Invariably, the stories came up disappointing. One man was a former biker who was now on his second wife, and though they had been married for some time, his children were from his first marriage and he never saw them and rarely cared to. He loved his current wife, but when he questioned himself on it he'd admit it was mostly because she smoked the same cigarettes he did and also liked Tullamore Dew and T-shirts and leather. But what more could you ask for, really? Especially at his age, and with the series of arrests in his youth, etc. They were traveling to a family reunion on her side of the ancestral tree and both were mildly enthused about the trip. At least they were getting away.

A woman and her two children sat a few chairs down from them. She was knitting. The kids sat playing quietly with each other. They would meet up with their father the following day (he'd been away somewhere on a months-long business assignment) and what was once routine (when he was home) would seem suddenly a fabulous vacation. I didn't quite have the energy, or the heart perhaps, to work out the details of the torrent affair that would blow up in his face upon his family's arrival—the result of a mixing up of dates on his calendar, I had thought—abandoning the tiresome work of creating that ugly tale in favor of returning to the First and Last Chance for more Guinness.

But barely had I stuffed the book into my backpack and hoisted the pack onto my shoulder when she arrived. She whirred in through the door by the tracks, accompanied by a lanky redheaded boy who wore large black plugs in the lobes of his ears. She bit into him with a sharp whisper—*frantic*. He mostly chuckled, casting a lazy arm to her elbow as she pushed ahead of him. She blew down the aisle between the last row of seats and came to an abrupt halt, as if mechanically checked from exiting the row. She looked around wildly, eyes darting to the other side of the room before her head had a chance to swivel and catch up.

—Where?! Where?! she spits, her hands stuffed deeply into the pockets of her bulky jacket. Her boyfriend mumbles something to her, still the bemused look on his face, offers again a guiding hand to her biceps. She spins from it and slants forward to the restroom, turning once halfway there to look back and squawk the requisite nonsense that causes him to follow. The pair disappears into the ladies' room.

I recline in my seat, propping left leg upon right to await their glorious return. It comes in less than 30 seconds. She leading the way out and immediately catching herself up in the bright lights of the vending machines. She studies the contents blankly for a moment, swimming through the clouds of her mind, then throws a quick jab to her boyfriend's stomach.

A barrage of glancing pops to his midsection follows, each blow accentuated by a screeched whisper —*Money! Money!* She grows more frantic at his negative response, slaps the arm of his coat back and forth with an open hand, then suddenly folds at the crease of her midsection, as if her stomach had just popped and evaporated —*Two fuckin' quarters, asshole! Two goddamned!* She turns, yanking at the sides of her tightly knit hat, and beelines for the door. A stream of profanity-laced desperation spews from her mouth, floating over the room like cigarette smoke. As if on cue, her hands dig into coat pockets, trying, I imagine, to shake loose her pack of smokes and a lighter. Shrieks blare from her throat at the inability to draw these items forth, but then she is suddenly able to do so. Through a series of shaking fits, her hands manage to guide a slightly bent cigarette to her lips, but she still struggles mightily in the operation of the lighter. Tremulous legs rattle her there in the spot. Her man approaches, takes the lighter and ignites the cigarette. He guides her by the arm out the door. Once out, though, she breaks free again and races off into the night, arms in a new flurry, mouth yelling soundless, legs tripping dangerously behind the slant of her torso. Her boy, ever grinning, lopes after.

—There'll be hot dogs, says the former biker's woman, patting him gently on the knee and smiling hungrily up at him. He nods back in pleasant accord. I hoist the backpack onto my shoulder and shoot through the exit just taken by Tristessa and her boy. *Tristessa!* (I laugh over the name now in the freeing night air)—the strung-out, gray-skinned, sad Billie Holiday-like beauty of Kerouac's Mexico, back here presently to haunt me. Immediately I'd felt some connection to her, but was unable to place her specifically till I myself was rushing away; only in fleeing those tired bodies in the train station does the name pop magically into my head. And now a swelling of sadness and regret replaces the thrill of recognition. She had come so far, was so close, as if we had both spilled into a courtyard of some labyrinth, and I'd let her go off again. Had I but placed her minutes earlier, I could now be tailing her literary path through the night—down back alleys, over pools of thick, gritty sludge, through drapes in doorways behind taco stands, into a mildewy back room where she and her redheaded boy are presently scoring vials of junk; could sit huddled close and watch their minds go smoothly in the sweat.

I console myself with the thought of my own imminent score. And perhaps now they'll be more life for me at the old saloon. The terrain passes less quickly underfoot returning than it did leaving the bar (what— twenty minutes, half an hour back?) the steps more labored, sidewalk as treadmill in spots. But, finally, I rise up over a curb and there she sits, small and ancient, truly the looking of a place one might dream of at sea, keeping her there in his mind's eye as a talisman, warding off death by giving his heart something real and solid to beat for.

There's a moment of panic as I come over the precipice and see the bar now lined with people. But my breath returns (once my head clears and focuses correctly) at the sight of my stool sitting there empty, awaiting my return. Leonard is not a bit surprised, starts me a fresh pint.

—Train was late getting out of Los Angeles, I explain to him nonetheless.

—Yeah, that happens.

—Better to wait here, than …

He nods, takes up his tin of chew and provides himself with a bit of it.

Howard (or whom I take to be Howard) has arrived during my absence and sits next to me engrossed currently in conversation with Helen, their murmurs barely audible above the music and din from the group in the corner, whose number has increased by three or four high-spirited professionals.

—Well, look who the cat drug in! Helen's voice is suddenly piercing, cuts into my chest, takes hold of my lungs and begins tugging. If I were the sort who couldn't control his temper, I'd get up and strangle her. I can't explain my new reaction toward her, for she hasn't changed from before—her voice and the intention in it are the same, tipsy and good-humored if a bit sardonic—but I hate her now. And when her companion turns all bloated and glassy-eyed, extending a thick, feeble hand to me, I struggle for the resolve to slap it away. But here is my hand now in his perspiry grip, being swallowed by its softness. And when he smiles broadly, all the angst of the previous moment is taken from me, soaked up into his large, wet body, where I feel it mingle pleasantly with a host of other pleasant toxins.

—Nice to meet you, I say, for I have already begun to wonder how I might write him.

He slurs a response and begins laughing.

—I told Howard all about you and your lonely ways, Helen injects, leaning back from the end of the bar.

Howard grins. —I know all kinds of ladies in the 50-and-above set I could call over for you. But then they've probably all gone to bed by now. He begins laughing before he can get all this out, the last few words coughed up from his belly in a phlegmy chuckle.

—No, I'm fine, I assure him. Helen doesn't know the full story on me.

—Whoaoooo …

—I know plenty just by looking. Plenty.

—I was just about to make my move on her, Howard. Then I heard her call you over.

—Oh shit my pants, I'm too much woman for you even if I am all withered away.

—Don't let me stop you, Howard chuckles belatedly.

And then it's quiet again, and everything begins anew. I'm sure I can hear the clock ticking. After some time, I come to see it as part of a system that's clandestinely draining my blood, with all the tubes invisible, and the whole of it operated by Leonard's stereo—the levels that dance on the receiver correspond to those of my heart and my brain and whatever else might be vital in me. Leonard is the young, disinterested, student operator—he's seen it all before, a thousand times, watched any number of men die right in front of him, siphoned off their lives for some incomprehensible profit, some scam, that even being eleven years his senior I can't get my mind around. But he takes it all in stride—another day's work—spits chew juice into his brown cup.

I have a sudden urge to aid him. That is, take up smoking again after several years off the habit and fill my lungs with volumes of gray smoke, eat myself up from the inside out. I can almost hear the crackle of my innards being taken already like wood by the termites—glorious cancer to spread and wipe out any ill feeling from a life lived, what, if not poorly, absentmindedly and too long.

—Era octubre, I whisper (though it is seven months shy, or five months going, for that). Nevertheless, I have let myself become as poor and as old and as honorably naïve as el coronel de García Márquez, awaiting my never-coming pension here at this bar. And perhaps, oddly enough, this depressive dream will save me for a while—for as long as I can continue to float on it and feel truly that I *am* of the same stuff as el coronel, and accept that my remaining days will be governed by nothing much other than piles and piles of mounting shit.

—Era octubre, I repeat.

—Cómo?

—Nada, Leonard. Otra Guinness por favor.

—Sí, viene enseguida.

The bus pulled into the one-story bus station that stretched burnt orange plaster and metal over a flat parcel on the brush-strewn outskirts of Guanajuato. The day was falling into twilight as I ducked into the front seat of a waiting cab.

—Cuál es la mejor cantina en la ciudad? was my pressing question to the driver.

—Cantina o bar?

—Qué es la diferencia?

—Pues, the cabbie demurred, directing his vehicle up a slight hill. Bars are what the young people go for, he said after a while. They have music, dancing, the like. That's what you want.

—Y cantinas?

—Sí, hay.

So I was on my own again, with the tour book supplying only a bit of guidance. Winding down the hill on foot from my hotel, spiraling down medieval, stone-walled streets in the dark that opened onto street-lamped, circular plazas crowded with people, I was just as well alone. The directions in the guide book useless, or my eyes useless, as I circled, finally, the town center, several levels farther down, no doubt looping many times past that darkened callecita I sought, the one the guide book promised would take me to the swing-door cantina of José Alfredo Jimenez's dreams. Better that I had struck out truly on my own, in which case I would've entered the very real cantina up the hill toward my hotel, and not been enticed to pass it by for the ideal sold me in the book. How much better, then, would have ended the night?

But happy once again and satisfied with my latest death plan, I turn and look to bum a smoke from Helen. Yet, ah! Look who it is—the apparition in the doorway! My beautiful, gaunt, desolation angel, who I thought had slipped away from me for good, after having come so close but an hour earlier—her own cigarette smoke drifting from nostrils as she peers like some wary animal into the small shack bar, her green hat knit down to large black marble eyes, which bounce now being caught by the light, her nose and cheeks and shoulders aquiver, her fingers trembling in the duty of her smoking. Only the dark, shoulder-length hair, drifting calmly in the evening's breeze, seems immune to the stress working on the rest of her body.

She spins from the door and locks her right forearm across her stomach to support the left's craning to lips with cigarette. She walks out of view, but returns shortly with her boy in tow. She discusses matters with him in a restraint that has pushed all the earlier arm-waving tension into her core, where it sends out a steady vibration to all points of her exterior, keeping it in a constant fray of electrical motion. The problem seems to be one over coming or not coming in. She looks then turns and walks away from the building, only to return and inch a bit closer than before. I half expect her to start pawing at the wood. The boy is unconcerned, perhaps a bit tired. He tells her something now and she again looks into the bar, her eyes maybe a touch calmer, her body less on edge, smoking her cigarette, considering all of us shades stuck inside.

Then she is gone. Her boyfriend remains in place awhile before turning and following, the first hint of annoyance or exasperation evident in his gait, or, to express it more accurately, in the pause just before he sets off. Light where the two had stood folds in on itself, revealing a too pure blackness and the sound almost of crickets chirping. The heavy curtain of which Tristessa now bursts through, gliding over the threshold and sailing across the floorboards in a line to the john at the shack's far end.

Her boy comes in and heads to the bar. He orders a beer and takes the stool next to mine (that which'd been left unoccupied sometime recently I don't remember). When the beer comes he cups his hands around the pint's rim and stares bemusedly at the wall behind the bar. Perhaps the knickknacks, the memorabilia, dance for him, acting out as in movie reel the history of the place. Perhaps smoke still drifts from pipes of sea dogs in oilskins. And tentacled waves crash over in his brain. Perhaps he still dreams at night of napping in a field of grass biting hayseed, where a childhood dog comes and still licks at his ankle. He takes a slow sip of his beer, then returns it again to the bar and holds it, pleasantness painted on his face.

Tristessa slips from the bathroom and saddles up next to him. She orders a beer, along with a shot of tequila with lime. The order comes and she abruptly throws back the shot and stuffs the lime into her teeth. She sneezes violently. Again. Commences to wiping her nose. Her eyes dart as before. Her boy laughs and tells her to drink her beer. She glares at him, but does as she's told, draining a good quarter of her beverage in a swallow. When she lowers the glass to the bar, her shoulders drop noticeably. She murmurs to him low. He smiles at first, then laughs and turns back to amuse himself with the clutter on the wall. Tristessa hunches in over her drink, staring down into the wood shelving that rises from the floor behind the bar to the height of Leonard's waist. Her eyes glaze, blinking clear only when she rediscovers her beer and takes a healthy draught from it. The eyes then fall dead again.

But she's spooked alive soon enough (by what, it's impossible to say) and turns true agitated fit to cruise like mad for the bathroom. Her boyfriend simply watches her go, quite happy to watch the door swing shut behind her. Then he's back to smiling at the wall, though perhaps with a turning down pinch of worry at the right corner of his lips this time. And with Tristessa gone, the room promotes a strange, tense feeling of relief from tension—all of us simply waiting, knowing an explosion will happen before long with this girl.

A bit later she reenters the stage and crosses it. But halfway out she misses her mark. And instead of returning to her stool, she bypasses it, continuing behind the backs of her boy and myself to collect a thick sampling from the napkins stacked just to the right of my elbow on the bar. Without thinking I turn and look at her. Her head draws up like a deer from a creek, eyes reflecting terror. If I were to make a move, the slightest flinch, she would—very un-deer-like—spring claws and lash off the better part of my face. I try to stay cool, still. But to do so, I mustn't take my eyes from hers, a constancy that triggers a silent mating dance, wherein paranoiac fear rattles the eyes in her sockets, while I try with soft look to caress her gaze into calmness, press as with thumbs her eyeballs and massage away the tension of junk (or the lacking of it). Still there remains a sense of horrific recognition and disbelief in her fear—that it is *me*, that I have somehow in this small, isolated cabin by the sea, after all our mad, but never quite so close, wanderings and graspings spinning twine around the earth, finally tracked her down. That we have been brought back together. A reunion of two strangers. Here I am, calmly, now that she is within my reach, now that I have her, nothing but time ticking gladly from the clock to allow me to slowly drop my net. If that be my goal.

I risk a smile and she darts.

Next to her at the bar even her boyfriend is awoken by her sudden retreat. He casts a wary (though not accusatory) eye in my direction, and I return the look with one of complete non-understanding—a disinterested neighbor sparked only by the awareness that this stranger has decided to look my way too. He accepts it as such and returns to study his partner, still visibly shaken, clutching her drink, end times playing in her eyes.

It is mad that she has wandered up this far, stayed this young, or was reborn somehow, waking in a morning after shooting up one night in the summer of 1957 to wipe roughly 50 years of crusted sleep from her eyes and step out through the gate at Orizaba 210 and head north in her stained white sleeping garment up the tree-lined streets of Mexico City's Colonia Roma, past the parks with their fountains spraying white in the morning's steady sun, past the gray copy of David, turning right on Chapultepec, then cutting down back streets to emerge sometime later under the shadow of the Palacio de Bellas Artes and on with knife at the draw through Plaza Garibaldi and beyond, till the city slowly steps its way out of the ancient valley, tracing a ledge up pine-ringed mountains, then slowly down again into dirt that, later, brings rows of finely planted green spikes that she traverses with walking stick and the newly acquired green hat (bought from a roadside tent or small shop wedged into a short line of buildings struck against the open landscape like an Old West movie set, announcing itself in loud candy colors) and with grit, drifting, never questioning this going, *but* going, drawn as Cacciato to her storied fate, finally (what—months later?) arriving North and crossing the border in the blazing haze of an afternoon sun to walk on how many hundreds of miles more to one day settle here in the nook of the bay and reacquaint herself with junk, to gather to herself the new century's fear of the forever coming bust (which in her confusion she may believe she has just found present in me—a cop, iceman, ghost) and the much older, greater, countering fear of *lack*, of intestine-pulling hunger for her drug's white comfort, legs to jelly in the strictures of an age-old prayer.

She retreats once more to the bathroom, spinning from her stool in such a flash of justnowrealized fright (the knowledge of what is about to be sprung on her finally coming clear to her maybe—I swear as she flees a hiss escapes her lips: *the writer!*—catching up with that first, unthought of dash from the danger of me—her animal quickness) that half her stack of napkins is taken up in the whirl and spreads out into five or six perfect white squares drifting soundless in a slow descent to the ancient, soot-covered floor, the squares tossed up occasionally by some unfelt breeze, jumping at odd, frantic angles before refinding their drift and sailing round in slow loops to safe landing away from the brush of human contact. Then Tristessa's man is off the stool himself and giving chase, likewise slow (to the dance of floating napkins) in his elongated steps (that if considered from a certain view seems the rush wound slowly only that one might see it, and if by another, a lazy parade as a matter of understood duty, with no concern but for satisfying that itch, whatever its origin, to be seen as the loyal companion—to simply do what's expected) stepping through the drifting napkins to arrive himself at the bathroom door just before it closes, reopening it with a swing of his arm to reveal Tristessa there before the mirror, fingers tight upon her face, stretching the flesh back from her cheekbones, horrified by the eyes returning her gaze without recognition, looking beyond her, in fact, to more interesting things, lifting to see over her shoulder, till her man comes and grips her by the shoulders and takes her to him, the mirror returning a proper, physically accurate reflection then, as the door recloses on the bronze of girl melting into her boy.

—You American? Monica asked on the patio of that American-style bar in Guanajuato's Jardín de la Unión, the one offering two-for-one domestics till 9 p.m.

—Yes.

—We're going dancing, she said.

But I shouldn't have.

The boy escorts Tristessa to her stool once again, his large hands steadying her shoulders from behind and moving her rusted automaton body by the force of his pushing weight, her knees clicking forward, ready to stick straight at any moment and make his job more difficult by dragging. But she manages the few final steps, then wrestles free of him to hoist herself onto the stool. The fury in her eyes orders another beer.

Leonard is concerned. You can almost see the sweat brewing on his forehead as he turns from giving Tristessa her beer and comes back down the bar, mumbling something in his mind. Shadows play under his skin—fear of what Tristessa might burst out and do at any moment; fear, then annoyance, at what he'll have to do to handle it; working the trouble the boyfriend might give when this happens, figuring it to be minimal, again an annoyance and perhaps a sore hand tomorrow if it comes off poorly, but that should be it; glancing me over a sec, wondering if I'd help, and, if I did, if I'd be more a help or a hindrance—he doesn't give away the answer, but walks past to the CD player and begins pushing buttons. And in the clicking of his nervous work, the atmosphere of disaster somehow subsides. A shadow comes and descends over the grouping of Tristessa and her man, dimming the edge of the two, confining them to exhaustion, where perhaps Tristessa will overheat and seize and finally lay herself out—or not—and wake tomorrow on some cool, moist sheets, open eyes to a second or two of hopefulness, of treading off in a confident new direction with none of the worries of the day before and all the days before that stacked precariously atop one another to weigh on her shoulders and mind. But then, in thinking them gone, she brings them back, and she'll slump to the soft mattress again, twist her hair up in her fingers and beg not to regain the energy that'll sit her up once more and send her out on the maddening search for the junk to uncoil her rusting soul.

The two of them—Tristessa and her boy—are harmless now, resting as a cold, hardened mass at the end of the bar.

And so the clock ticks, and I spin my way through a couple more pints, feeling myself drug deeper and deeper into the warm bath of 'em. I feel the shadow of lethargy moving down the bar for me (now that it's fairly petrified the boy and Tristessa) and decide it is time for me to remove myself from its path before it's too late. I settle for a second time with Leonard and he knows this time it is final. He takes my hand, wishes me a good trip. I thank him, give a parting wave to Howard and Helen (and wonder how many of me they are waving back to) and slip out through the open door into blackness. I will wait in the train station for half an hour more, occupying the same fiberglass chair that I had used earlier, staring across at the same Segal travellers sitting wrapped in their blue and red plaster. I'll board the train just before midnight, and make it to the lounge car with enough time yet before it closes to order a beer, then half a bottle of wine. And by longing for Tristessa, I will push off until morning that ever-nagging desire to kill myself.

II

La Línea

In my delirium I wandered deep beneath the ground through a thousand of these dens, and behind locked doors of iron I suffered and died a thousand deaths.

—Jack London, *John Barleycorn*

… WHICH I SHOULD IF I WAS GOING BACK TO MEXICO, AS IT WAS NOT A DECISION made without some trepidation. Perhaps it stemmed from all the stories in the news and the books I'd read about the Mexican drug wars, the ultraviolence, the absurdity, where violence now begets violence and the road back to the source, the rationale (however demented it was to begin with) is obscured by the vast pools of blood drained from forgotten bodies and from the dense smoke of grinding hatred. Now you kill just to kill because it's what's done. It's the order of things.

So that probably had me a bit on edge. But there was more to it than that. I was more frightened, more skittish, generally. Even while sitting at home, my skin would vibrate with a certain unclassifiable dread that only music or drink or sleep might manage to smooth into a tolerable evenness. I was averse to travel. But once I got moving I generally felt better. The rush of the airport reloaded me with needed energy (though also with pounds of nervous gas bubbling in my stomach). And zipping through the crushing city—el monstruo—in a taxi seemingly bent on self-destruction flushed all anxiety not-of-the-moment out of my pores. But in the hotel in the evening as the orange sky out the window burned off in the smog, or afterwards in the complete blackness, the dread would return and I'd find myself wishing I'd stayed home, that I had never become foolishly excited by the prospect of search and discovery and spontaneously booked the flight to come here and hastily made arrangements to meet up with that woman I knew only as B, who I hoped could supply me with a good deal of the information I was looking for. At least with a good start.

Still, it is somewhat better, now, sitting here outside the café, smoking. Though it will be worse again later once the nicotine buzz wears off. B will come and we'll discuss the matter of Tristessa and Esperanza, but I'll be depressed later and won't know how to rid myself of it.

It was at that moment, I believe, waiting for B outside the old Café de Ángel on la calle Pilares, that I, a confirmed atheist, decided that I must, after all, make the pilgrimage to Chalma, despite the absurdity of the place, to see for myself the Santuario del Señor, that church that had drawn Esperanza Villanueva and her husband David Tesorero and even William S. Burroughs to its enclosure, to its waters that run through stone-fashioned streams in professed holiness, to its dry concrete paths paved to grind penitent knees into sacred oblivion.

I light the cigar, a Te Amo Aniversario torpedo, sit back in the white plastic chair and exhale a cloud of gaily antagonistic smoke. The practice akin to the bull's snort, the lion's growl that bubbles freely from his skin. I am here. There's always the sense of trouble, but nobody wants that. Let me save it for my writing. B will be here soon. And after we've finished talking and have exchanged the requisite papers, I might well be armed with all the information I need to write an adequate portrait of Esperanza Villanueva, whom Kerouac had fictionalized as his Tristessa, then left and never rediscovered. Though the goal is more than adequate portrait, isn't it? I would like to paint her with all the full, abrasive color of life. Of living. To fill in the long, blank stretches of nothingness on either side of that ink-washed passage from 1955 through 1956 when Jack was with her. The blankness that all those scholars, all those writers before me who took an interest in Kerouac and wrote volumes analyzing his life and his work, never managed to fill. Or cared to fill. Had Esperanza vanished so completely after Jack was through with her? Had she erased her path leading up to him so successfully that it was forever after untraceable? Or had all those who sought to cast a new, unique look on the travels of Kerouac simply not cared to see this woman other than through Jack's gaze? Was this drug-addled, prostituting Azteca deemed a distraction from the greater task of understanding the American writer? Was she not worth the trouble? Or did her trails running away from Jack—into the past and into the future—only expire into the thin Mexican air, leaving anyone foolish enough to take up the search fanning silken particles of light? But I will begin it, I tell myself, happily smoking my Te Amo in the sun outside the Café del Ángel, which itself no longer exists. I can start the story after B arrives and supplies me with all the requisite information.

A piece of tobacco leaf cracks loose from the roll and bends back to blazingly test an unfelt breeze. The teenage boy who works in the café jogs across la calle Pilares, wrapping the ties of his apron about his waist.

—Cómo estás?

—Bien. Y tú?

—Muuuuuy bien, he grins.

I wave to him as he passes into el Ángel, then watch as his form dissipates in the white glare of the café's front glass. I inhale slowly and breathe smoke. I wash the throat with café americano, igniting the residual trail of tobacco juice. There is plenty of time to wait for her.

In her 1994 Kerouac biography, Ann Charters tells us that Esperanza Villanueva was born in Juárez. Ten years later, Kerouac biographer Paul Maher, Jr. places Villanueva's birth in Southern Texas and says she attended high school in Carrizo Springs.

A Chevy rolls past.

The sun is out.

Wind rustles the trees down the street behind me.

Ellis Amburn, in his 1999 book *Subterranean Kerouac: The Hidden Life of Jack Kerouac*, makes the claim that Jack and Esperanza had sex 56 times over the course of 42 days, a ludicrous calculation even for a healthy couple, let alone for an alcoholic and a morphine addict who freely laced their wasted days with marijuana and secanols too. In his novel, Jack says they never fucked, but later admitted in an interview with Ted Berrigan for the Paris Review that he did finally get his "little no-good piece." Barry Miles writes that Esperanza later married a policeman.

And now the breeze blows past. Though, in fact, it has been nearly ten years since it went by. The Café del Ángel in Colonia Del Valle later replaced by Restaurante Pocillo, now shielded by metal shades drawn down over its windows as I look at it. Painted words in script advertise Pizza y Pasta, Café y Desayuno. Date el gusto.

Yet despite the gap of years, a regular neighborhood character still emerges from a side street and approaches the couple sitting two tables over from me outside el Ángel. He's outfitted in a white fútbol jersey with matching shorts—he has a different team's jersey for each day of the week, and probably more. He joins the others, reclines in the open seat, snaps left leg over right and immediately starts in talking, as if picking up the thread of a conversation abandoned midstream a day or two earlier. Soon he is laughing and smoking a cigarette.

It will be different with B, no doubt. More formal. Perhaps she'll tote an attaché case or a messenger bag, sit and draw forth papers, which she'll hand over to me. I will consult them sternly, nodding at the appropriate moments. Very good, nice, I might say as I puff away at my cigar. This is exactly what I need. Yes. Exactly. Thank you very much. Muchísimas gracias.

—It was the least I could do, she'll say, casting a nervous glance to the street.

Of course, she'll want something in return. Some tit for tat, or am I still thinking in terms of violence? She has never specified what it is she is looking for from me. All our correspondence conducted via e-mail. Vague references to an equally beneficial exchanging of ideas. Something to advance her career. But in the end, will something more concrete be in order? Cold, capitalistic cash, instead of lofty notions of intellectual fair trade? Or will our negotiations trend more nebulous? Fall in line with the scheme perpetrated by Monica those years back in Guanajuato, whatever that may have been or if the scheme ever did, indeed, exist outside of my own weary, paranoid calculations. Am I completely incapable of trusting people now?

I inhale smoke from the cigar. My brain more active on smoke. For an hour or two, at least, after which time it will predictably begin to crash, taking the rest of my system down with it. I'll get jittery, then depressed, and tomorrow I'll have a hole in my stomach. Still, after some time—a week, maybe, or a month or two—I'll again find cigars inviting and will light up another with all romanticized expectation.

The fútbol fanatic is ever jovial, pointing now to the woman at his table with the lit end of his cigarette, just before smashing it out in the ashtray. He is laughing, as are the other two at his table. —Sí, he repeats, sí. Exactamente. Exactamente así.

—Nooooo, is the woman's drawn-out reply, moaned long and low and cheerfully disintegrating into a fit of giggles.

—Siempre, the man concludes, reclining in his chair with a satisfied grin set to his lips.

B may not be coming. I realize this now. She is currently 15 minutes late. I hadn't even considered the possibility that she might stand me up. From the moment we made the arrangements via e-mail, I had the event chiseled into the future. I would leave my room and walk the few blocks to the café. (Although, of course, I would not do this, as I no longer rented the room that I had ten years earlier, but must now travel from my hotel in Colonia Roma, taking the Metrobús down Insurgentes to the stop at Parque Hundido.) She would arrive. I'd quickly review the information she brought and we'd discuss it—either in cursory fashion or at some length. Then we would part, amicably, excitedly, resignedly, with a future meeting arranged or not. But it never occurred to me that she might not show at all, a possibility that now, suddenly, as the content from our e-mail exchanges lights in my brain with the heightened sizzle of a steer brand, each letter, each word, each sentence burning with the full intensity of its (now altered) meaning, seems—and always should have seemed, I suppose—the most likely conclusion to our story. In fact, I can no longer say for certain that she'd even suggested a meeting. Again I have been foolish. The mind takes so long to learn certain things. It may never learn certain things.

He'll be back soon, Esperanza thought, sitting in the narrow band of yellow light that lay draped over the small kitchen table, her hands gripping a white porcelain mug at the table's center, though much of the cup's heat had already dissipated. She sipped the tea. It was just after four. He'd be home soon if he didn't stop at the bar. If he did, he wouldn't be home till much later, and might not make it home at all, which, she conceded, would be preferable. It would be easier to work.

She finished the tea and took the empty mug over to the sink. Placing it there on the sink's stained white enamel surface felt a bit like snapping a final piece into a puzzle—the cup with its brown-splotched interior and wet dusting of spent tea leaves completing a multilayered picture of excremental disgust. She turned away from it and went out through the screen door to the concrete drive for a smoke. The street beyond the heavy metal gate at the driveway's end was empty and silent. She took the pack of cigarettes from her sweater pocket, helped herself to one and lit it.

When they first moved into the house, years earlier, shortly after they were married, their main concern was over the noise. The street was full of young couples like themselves and teemed with small children who crisscrossed the blocks of concrete and strips of pavement in orchestrated patterns of coursing energy, punctuated by unchecked squeals and yelling and the clatter of kicked metallic objects. Young, grinning faces would lift into windows at all sunlit hours, becoming, before long, automatic accouterments of a home's construction.

—Shoo! her husband barked at the tiny round face that popped into the bedroom window one morning shortly after they had moved in. But the face merely grinned, then lost itself to laughter watching the man's ample backside press and release in its motion. —Váyate, ranita!

She rubbed the cigarette out on one of the thick bars of the metal gate and returned to the house. She'd successfully killed 10 minutes. If he wasn't home soon, she could start laying the complex out on the kitchen table. Otherwise she'd keep it in the bedroom or haul it into the bathroom and keep the door shut. Surely, though, he already knew about it. He must. Still, it was best, she thought, to maintain their unspoken agreement of secrecy. He wasn't coming home tonight, though. She felt it now. More and more, in fact, he'd been coming home less and less. He was at work during the day, going here and there about the city, poking into God knows what rancid holes of existence (and death—mostly death, after all) then drifted to the bar directly after, or directly after dinner, and caroused till late into the night, when he'd finally come home and insert his mindless form into the bed's rumpled sheets. Sometimes she was there, sometimes she was not. They didn't talk about it.

He was at the door now.

Entering, he strips out of his police jacket and hangs it on the hook by the door. He leaves the shoulder holster on and comes over and kisses her on the cheek.

—Amor.

—I didn't think you were coming.

He shows her a nicotine-stained grin, but says nothing.

—I'm not sure what we'll have. Maybe there's still some ham and bread. We could reheat the soup.

—Amor, he grins.

—Amor, amor. She pushes past him. I want to eat.

—Dentro de un poco me voy al Culo de Tigre, he says as if reminding her of a previously discussed appointment.

She lifts herself from the fridge.

—Of course. (Siempre.) She exhales. —OK, claro.

He pushes a grin into the tight flesh of his cheeks.

—Are you eating then or no? she asks.

After he went, Esperanza took the shoebox from the closet and brought it out to the kitchen table. She removed the lid and took the bunch of plastic baggies from within and tugged off the rubber band holding them together. She placed the baggies on the table. Then she removed the large bag filled with the special complex and set it beside the baggies. She returned the lid to the box and set the box aside on one of the table's peg-leg chairs. She portioned out the large bag's contents into the small baggies, filling each of them halfway. She would weigh them later, as always, and, as always, be raked over the coals for it.

—Take a goddamned scale home with you already, Borges would chide her upon spying her there again beneath the florescent tubes in his basement, weighing out the baggies of complex. You'll mix things up one of these times.

—My husband will find it.

—Bullshit. He'd be afraid to even look for it. He doesn't want to know about this.

—He already knows.

—He suspects something. But he doesn't know. How could he, really? Not this. But even if what we're doing were within his scope of understanding, he wouldn't want to know about it.

She frowns.

—I don't want it in my home, she tells him.

—As you wish. But you're gumming up the works.

She giggled then, or would, hearing another of the charming anachronisms so at odds with her boss's line of work. She'd laughed in spite of herself hearing about the night in the alley behind el Culo de Tigre when Borges whacked Daniel Ovida and the poor kid's brains bounced off the place's brick backside to splatter all over Borges' Peter Millar wool trousers and Barker Black shoes with the ostrich cap toes.

—Durn burn his hide! Borges yelped, futilely brushing the wet gray matter from his thighs. Durn burn his hide!

—It's only that it troubles me, her husband, Marco, said, scarfing down a ham sandwich. I worry about you.

—You needn't.

—But you know I do, he said, smiling warmly and mindlessly showing her the clumps of wet bread wadded between his teeth.

—You needn't.

He stared at her a bit, allowing his black eyes to drip their full complement of liquid dog pity. But he said nothing more about it. And soon he was wiping his lips on his sleeve and pushing back from the table.

—I'll try not to be late, he said just before the door whacked shut behind him.

Her father would leave like that, with the wooden screen door in her childhood home clapping stingingly against its wood frame each time he exited into the night. She never saw him come home on such nights. But he was there in the morning always, like any other day, though he might give just a glimpse of himself as he pushed on his straw hat and headed to the fields without a word to anyone. But at the midday meal he was sweaty and jovial again, and by evening, his eyes at half-mast, he'd grin over his tortillas with a sleepy contentment and hum endearments to his brood of children. Several evenings would pass then before the screen door would whack shut again, casting her father out into that unknown world of adult blackness.

She went out through the white metal gate and headed west along la calle José Borunda. Her shoulder ached already from the heavy downward pressure of the canvas messenger bag, the strap digging into the soft spot just outside the joint. Her shoulder had felt fine the past couple of days without the weight on it. But the instant she took up the strap again the pain swelled as if she'd been carrying the bag all the while. At Perú she turned right, passing under the honey mesquite and hackberry trees that lined the sidewalk, up past the Chinese restaurant, crossing over Avenida 16 de Septiembre and past the gated, bucolic palace on the corner, past the foreign bank, then left on Ignacio Zaragoza. And as she passed down that way, with the row of crumbling façades announcing their sickness as sudden white patches inflamed in the blackness, she thought, as she always did passing along this part of the route, of that long-ago name she herself had employed—Zaragoza—as she walked streets not much different than these (though there was more a stench of rotted vegetation and spent feces in the air then, replaced now by a much wilder press of doom, buzzing cross black wires in the night's taut screen as if broadcasting an incessant whir of amplified insect torture) where she turned tricks to keep the money coming in, or the drugs coming in—the money flipped directly to keep the drugs coming in—Zaragoza—and they'd breathe it in her ear as they came, almost crying.

—You're late. I wondered if you were coming.

She slipped through the half-open door and ducked beneath Ramón's outstretched left arm.

—Cut the drama, she said. Let's finish this. I want to sleep tonight.

He closed the door and followed her down the narrow, darkly paneled hall, admiring her taut backside as she hurried along. What a wonderful gift it would be to a pair of curious hands. But she knew how it tempted, bobbing in Hellenistic response to her legs' purposeful marching. A bitch like that knew, all right. Can you imagine how she tortures that fat fuck of a drunken, copper husband with that ass of hers? Dropping a towel from it after a shower, just to show him, I bet, just to swell his tongue with thoughts of licking the sparkling beads of moisture from the flesh's perfection. Then withholding it from him. Poor fat fuck. No wonder he's a lush. Yes, she knew all right. And how far divorced she is now from that past life of hers. That sunken, wafer-thin life, trolling the backstreets of DF. And how much thinner still and more wasted she must've seemed then propped against the ballooning wheel well of a late-forties Mercury. Or is that how they scored in those days? And were there many Mercurys in Mexico then? Kerouac doesn't tell us. The action is all in tight adobe huts with barn animals prowling the grounds and drug-infused wonder and horror as Jack pops in and out of the higher-plane nexus of Catholicism and Buddhism, that as much as anything pushed him out into the rain-pelted streets of La Lagunilla that one, storied night to trek long concrete path through San Juan de Letrán home to his Raskolnikov-like perch in Colonia Roma atop the apartments at Orizaba 210. She doesn't think I know about all that. But I do. Ramón knows, honey.

She opened the basement door and continued down the steps in the dark. He flipped on the light.

—You'll trip and break your neck. Then where will we be? he called after her. I'd have to shoot you. Like a horse.

She didn't respond, or look back. She flicked the basement's light switch at the bottom of the stairs and disappeared around the corner.

Like a horse. Which wasn't, sadly, any exaggeration. What else could he do? Call the paramedics? Even hauling her to the hospital himself and dumping her at the entrance would be too risky. And be torture for her, really. No, one bullet to the back of the head would do it and it'd be over. Aside from the cleanup, of course, which is always more of a hassle than you want it to be. There'd be scrubbing and bleaching, and still the smell never really goes away (if, maybe, it's only there in your head). And he'd have to dump her, which would be a good hour or two driving, and some digging, perhaps, depending on what was available, and the stupid complications that always arise with bystanders. The number of 70-year-old ladies who go out at 3 a.m. to walk their dogs is off the charts! Or maybe it's just that one night they do it—the one night you need them *not* to—God or some other invisible force pulls these hags out of bed with the insistence that little Bonbon simply must urinate at that moment or he'll explode. The poor pooch dragging behind them on the leash more often than not, wishing he was still back in the warmth of his bed, such is the lunacy driving these witches out into the streets to mess up your plans. Their reward too often is a chunk of metal in the brain, and then you have two bodies to do something with and a yapping dog to kick down the street. How much nicer if Esperanza would just offer up that sweet ass of hers—share the love a bit, sister—and we could both forget for a while all the ugliness of this business. All the ugliness of living. Let me shoot off my horse cock, baby, not be a cock that shoots you like a horse. Ha ha! What say you? Then, maybe, holding you, subdued in my arms, I'd lovingly coax the past out of you. How 'bout it? "Tomorrow we may die, so we are nothing," isn't that what you used to say to Jack?

So he went, down the steps into the basement, the slippery coils of his brain lit with mirth. But upon completing his descent and turning the corner at stairs' end, he was just able to register a flash of recognition before the hook of a crowbar sank into his skull, relieving his prefrontal cortex of all thoughts of sexual domination and murder and biographical discovery and casting them together in one animated red arc out, over and down into the twisted fibers of the room's woefully outdated shag.

If Jack could see me now, she thought, passing again under the dark, fragrant leaves that danced so thoughtlessly above the sidewalk. Fellaheen no more, surely. Or would he rationalize it somehow? More of my *seekness*. The grand journey to enlightenment. No doubt, he would. He was always full of such bullshit, seeing the lighted spirit and Buddhist significance in everything. That all existence was strung together in a humming web of tremulous, torturous energy, sputtering by starts and fits toward its white explanation, its holy conclusion. Bull*shit*. But didn't we all function that way? In that previous life. My heavy devotion to Christ and his sacred virgin progenitor—especially to the Virgin, after all, my ignorant guadalupanismo—that I bore in the very molecules of my waxen blood. The hot drip of penance. The burning sacrifice scraped from knees on the stones at Chalma. Didn't we all wedge our minds into that holy vice? Didn't we revere it? Didn't we slice ourselves open repeatedly trying to relieve the inner pressure only to find it grow stronger? Didn't I receive Communion like sucking dick? Always on bended knee. Always in supplication. Always swallowing the warm ejaculate of Catholic suffering. And the glory that was to come. Well, Jack's Mexican Fellaheen girl was dead, sorry to tell him. (If she ever really existed.) I've been resurrected, Jack, as something quite apart from my former self. Something spawned again from dirt, as before, but demanding nothing from it this time. Expecting no deliverance. No holy command. Now simply being. Which, as it turns out, is anything but simple. But no matter. A person followed her course. She did the best she could. She kept her chin up and didn't get lost in wild expectations. For, in the end, what good were any of them? You wanta see expectations? Go check out that poor grab-ass Ramón.

The cab dropped me at the Casa de la Condesa, where I checked in and deposited my bags, splashed some water on my face, then headed out immediately to visit the Pegaso bookstore in the Casa Lamm, a grand house completed in 1911 at the corner of Orizaba and Obregón and now a cultural center with a café and space for concerts, art shows, banquets and various other events. I had frequented the bookstore a decade earlier when I lived in the city, passing hours in its various rooms of books on each of my visits.

The place was closed now. Though I hoped it was just for the day and wouldn't be locked up throughout my stay or, above all, hadn't gone out of business altogether. Judging by the heavy machinery stationed in the courtyard, there was construction underway on some part of the complex. I walked up and back along Obregón hoping to find some entrance to the bookstore I hadn't noticed earlier (or hoping that one would suddenly, magically appear) or that I might see a sign in a window or near the locked gate that would explain the situation to me. But nothing presented itself.

After a few additional minutes loitering, I finally relented and turned away from the building's opulent stone columns and expansive yet welcoming yellow walls and wandered into Obregón's broad median where the weekend market was in full flourish. I stopped and browsed through some books at various tables, but neither my heart nor head was in it, as I remained troubled by the locked gate at the Casa Lamm. I sorted through some old photos at another table—mostly pictures from the Mexican Revolution and of Hollywood and Mexican movie stars—hoping against all logic that I might uncover some stray shot of Tristessa. That is, that I would flip up a photo of Esperanza Villanueva in braids and sunglasses, walking the streets of Colonia Roma in the 1940s or '50s. She wouldn't be the subject of the photo, I suspected, but rather reside on the periphery, staring out from history at anyone observant enough to pick her out from the crowd and once again highlight her stride, as Jack had done so many years back. This was the other possibility I allowed myself—the excuse to continue flipping through the images—that perhaps there would be a shot of Kerouac or of Burroughs (who shot and killed his wife only blocks away from where I was then standing) in the stack, and that Esperanza would be there lingering at the corner of the frame, a fuzzy woman neither addressing nor avoiding the camera, quite content to be lost to the grainy brush of mid-twentieth-century photography. It was at least plausible. The stacks of photos might, in fact, hold pictures of the Beat writers in Mexico (there were several images, for example, of the Beatles and the Rolling Stones). But, after 10 minutes or so flipping through the piles of photos, the plausibility of finding Esperanza there seemed more of a stretch. I kept looking for a while, nevertheless, but finally put down the stack in my hand, gave a nod to the attendant at the table and moved on.

I headed north again, crossing back over the westbound lane of Obregón and continuing the few blocks to the Plaza Rio de Janeiro, circled past the gray copy of Michelangelo's David perched there amidst the fountain and went on one block more to the Casa Universitaria del Libro, another opulent, neocolonial residence from the early twentieth century situated at the intersection of Orizaba and Puebla, and now a building of the Universidad Nacional Autónoma de México, dedicated to the advancement and promotion of literature.

Unfortunately, this place was closed too on Sundays. So I made an appointment with myself to return another day and doubled back, retracing my steps over the handful of blocks to the intersection with Obregón, where I turned right to go check out the neighboring used bookstores I remembered from previous visits: A Través del Espejo and Librería Ático. El Espejo, likewise, was closed (again because it was the Lord's day) so I ducked into el Ático and quickly latched on to its line of shelves, sliding along them as if on a rail, trying to bring to mind all the titles or authors I had at some point thought I should look for upon returning to Mexican bookstores, and that now were sinking into the fog-laden bog of my mind. Names like César Aira, Carlos Fuentes and Roberto Bolaño came back rather easily. Others, such as Juan García Ponce and Alfonso Reyes, crept up through the muck at a more depressing rate. But when I saw the shelf sign Psicología I was instantly reminded of my desire to look for something by Erich Fromm, who had spent many years teaching, writing and conducting studies in Mexico. My eye first caught *El arte de amar*, one of his best-selling books. He wrote it here in Mexico in 1956, which I found appealing, as that was the same year that Jack was here with Esperanza, but the topic (as I formulated it from the book's title) didn't sufficiently draw me in. Certainly not enough to warrant the 112-peso price tag. Next to it on the shelf was *El miedo a la libertad*, his breakout book from 1941, which I had already read in the original English. But third in line stood *Budismo zen y psicoanálisis*, a thin, yellow paperback volume written by Fromm and D.T. Suzuki, the Buddhist scholar who had brought many in the West to Buddhism, including Fromm himself and the Beat poet Gary Snyder, who, in turn, instructed Kerouac and Allen Ginsberg. I took the volume from the shelf. Suzuki's half of the book was more or less a written version of the lecture he gave at the weeklong seminar on Buddhism and psychoanalysis in Cuernavaca that Fromm had arranged in the summer of 1957. Judging by a quick flip through this portion of the book, it appeared that Suzuki discussed the split between East and West, Unconsciousness and Consciousness, Art and Science, etc. On page 23 this line jumped out at me: "La naturaleza es caótica en el sentido de que es una reserva de posibilidades infinitas."

In his 70-page conclusion to the book, Fromm attempted to stitch together the lines of thought guiding Buddhism and psychoanalysis. Perhaps not surprisingly, if disappointingly, this seemed to lead him into occasional religious waxing, as on page 96, where he writes: "El fin de la vida es nacer plenamente, aunque su tragedia es que la mayoría de nosotros muere antes de haber nacido así." After an hour or so of additional browsing, I bought this book for 85 pesos, along with Fuentes' *La muerte de Artemio Cruz*, which had eluded me for too long ($115), and Juan Rulfo's *El llano en llamas* ($50).

I took these finds around the corner to the Café de Carlo, where, unfortunately, I had to accept a table inside (the three outside tables, as I was to learn over the coming days, being highly coveted spots that were rarely left vacant). The young waitress brought me the double-sided laminated menu. Though short and slight of build, she had large black eyes and a full face and seemed to look upon me with suspicion. I took the menu from her and flipped it over a few times, skimming the various offerings. I had no intention of ordering anything other than a café americano, but when the waitress returned, I asked also for a piece a pie imposible, which seemed to fill out the otherwise insubstantial order. She retrieved the menu, repeated the order back to me, asked if I'd like anything else, then went off to punch the order into the computer. I took the Fromm/Suzuki book from the store's plastic bag and flipped to page 85, where Fromm's piece on psychoanalysis and Zen Buddhism began. I read 10 pages or so there at the café, then completed the rest of it the next day on the bus riding to and from Chalma.

~

The house felt a fit of panic. That was the diagnosis Leon Trotsky scribbled in his journal later on that day that the wall in his study rippled. He'd been seated at his desk working in the early afternoon of a normal, sunny, late-spring day, the Ediphone faithfully scratching his dictation into its wax cylinder as he labored through an especially bothersome chapter of the Stalin biography they were paying him to write. He paused a moment, sighed, stared (rather longingly, he concluded, writing about it later) at the wall across from him, and, as if in response, the faded rose plaster swelled near the ceiling and ran as a smooth wave down the length of the wall where it was quietly swallowed by the floorboards. A moment of complete silence followed—a moment that nonetheless allowed for several minutes' worth of quiet browsing, during which the Old Man successfully cataloged a host of details particular to that moment in the room's history, particulars he consulted later while documenting the event in his journal, shuffling through the array like a stack of evidentiary photographs. Then came a large crash from somewhere far away, perhaps from the guard quarters, and a shock of energy set the home alive again, reanimating it with the noise of human motion.

He'd been in the house just over a week and remained skeptical of its suitability. His fatigue on this day had likely caused his doubts to become manifest, which is to say his fears had brought on hallucination, which is to say he was (as those diseased pragmatists the Americans would have it) quite possibly losing his marbles. But really he mustn't become ill again. There was too much at stake. And his failure at this critical hour could mean not only his own demise (his fall from grace, by fact, having commenced more than a decade earlier already; so here, demise, by all ends, referred most concretely to his death), but the life of his poor wife Natalia, as well, and young grandson Seva when he—*should* he—arrive, and not to mention the guards, typists, drivers, et al. who so bravely risked breath and limb to keep steady their Old Man's health and thereby maintain in good humming order their collective machine. Ah, but not a machine, hmm? No, that was Stalin's operation—that self-styled Man of Steel—not Trotsky's. Still, the Old Man and his crew were surely moving forward—inevitably, scientifically, as the dialectic ensured. They might fracture here and there, like this house, but the heart of the movement couldn't be stilled—it would stretch ever forward to claim that future settlement of historical fact. The house might be unsafe as it stood now, the outer and upper structure might give way in spots and crumble before the coming storm. But the foundation was strong. After all, it was nature itself, hurtling toward its conclusion. And, owing to that, this was the only place for the Old Man to be now. And the security, they assured him, would only improve.

The door to the study swung open and O'Brien leaned in.

—You okay?

—Fine, yes, fine, I said, absently brushing the sides of my denim jacket as if I'd been blasted with some powdery fallout from the audible disturbance. What happened?

—We're looking into it, O'Brien said before ducking out of the room again, leaving the door slightly ajar in his wake. With a huff I lifted myself from the chair to go reclose it. But first (and with an extra exhalation, I must admit) I corralled the Ediphone's tube, which must have fallen from my grip during the commotion and been left to sway a few inches above the floor. I set it back atop the machine, and the clip received the tube in a manner all too familiar and disturbing—with a click that sucked the apparatus home. A forgotten hand suddenly wrestled my stomach. Once again I was hanging up that cursed phone in Pachuca. I immediately shook the awful memory from my mind.

Some might be inclined to say that I had produced that movement earlier in the wall; that I had drawn it forth with the pure conviction of my thought. I admit that I considered the fading plaster with something akin to affection— affection that, in the several hours that have passed since the event, I have not yet been able to reconcile. Perhaps it was the first warm and gentle expression I had received from this house since moving in. Perhaps my justly skeptical armor had finally been pierced—the first bit of evidence that I might find, if not complete security, then at least some semblance of comfort within these walls—that I might be safe enough to write and carry on the other duties that have been laid upon my shoulders; might love my wife and build a satisfactory—if not satisfying—family life with our grandson when he arrives. In the rose walls I had perhaps glimpsed the possibility of a future not ruled by fleeing, by barricades and guns.

Yet, had not the wall rippled? Was it not panic? So the house—that is, the projection of my psyche into the dead materials of this latest holding pen—was hardly revealing itself the confident barer of glad tidings. The fleeing has not stopped. Stalin has not stopped. As I feed the words of his life to the Dictaphone, his arms grow and stretch around from the other side of the globe, fingering the poison he spilled into Lenin's blood. Even now the pulse in my veins quickens and pounds with the taste of his venom. Once again the fever rises on my brow. How many times can I cycle through it? How many times can I spin past death's door or traipse by that hallway leading to insanity and not be sucked in? How long can I continue to work?

- Sunlight caught by the door's leaded glass spread even and white, and inflamed the window's gold diamonds.
- Five books stood tilted against a stronger volume in the upper right nook of the yellow bookcase.
- There were three stacks of paper on the desk before me, my pen discarded atop the pile in the center.
- The desk lamp sat dormant.
- The wall was unbearably—achingly—flat after it rippled.

It was all too similar, really. Just the other evening O'Brien had stuck his head in through the open patio door and announced to me and my wife and a few others still seated at the dining room table:

—There's a call down the street for Natalia. On the Mexicana line.

Had the GPU already learned that this new house's phone line is an Ericsson? Or was it just luck? A 50/50 shot by Stalin's henchmen to draw the Trotsky vermin out from behind its walls through the hassle of a conflicting phone line.

Did they think they could get us that easily?

And now—today—the letter arrives. Anonymous, of course. Proposing that the Seva that was on his way to us might not be himself even, but perhaps some other kid shuffled in to take his place, or—worse—the genuine article, but with his young brain tickled into turning against his new caretakers: taught how to creep to his dear granddad's bed and slice a final snore from the old man's throat.

O'Brien was at the door again.

—There's a young man at the gate asking for you. A painter of some sort, I believe. Says his name is Ramón.

—Ramón?

—Yes, sir.

—Well what does he want then?

—Says he'd like to speak with you?

—Yes, of course. And no doubt his paintbrushes speak with poisonous darts.

—Would you like me to break them? O'Brien grinned.

An interesting thought. Haul all the lad's sticks out of his rucksack, snap them in two and toss them in a pile at his feet. A humorous thought.

—Is he well off? (That question raised the eyebrows on O'Brien's forehead, you can be sure.)

—Can't say. I don't think so. But I wouldn't say he's destitute, either.

—What does he want?

—He has some canvases with him. Maybe he's looking to sell you a few.

Wouldn't surprise me if he has the gall to ask to paint your portrait.

—My portrait?! The Old Man couldn't restrain a chuckle. It's getting a bit late on in the century for that kind of thing, isn't it? Doesn't this lad know that as we speak they're bombing Europe's bucolic meadows?

—I didn't ask him, sir.

—Well, do so then, the Old Man snapped through a creeping grin.

—With pleasure. And O'Brien was gone.

A painter. This whole cursed land is filled with painters. Diego, Frida, José Clemente … I can't shake myself of painters. Only Siqueiros has eluded me. Or is this him here now, banging on my door with canvases and a code name? That dirty Stalinist thug, Siqueiros. Best to level him in his tracks if he ever does show his face around here. But even he's not that brash and stupid. Perhaps Diego sent this Ramón—to observe firsthand the sorry state of my new environs; to report back so the bug-eyed round man can gloat over the news. And later, no doubt, he'll work a caricature of my frail personage into some mean-spirited public mural or other. Cuckolded cabrón! I'm done being painted!

—The past is the present, I told her over the phone from Pachuca. The past is the present. True enough. But what a thing to say to her. If that boy staffer of hers kept appearing from 1918, to tempt her once more with his affections, it was myself—Trotsky—who was inviting him. Hoping, obscenely, and against any statement I might make aloud—certainly any pronouncement yelled over a shitty public telephone—that this boy might indeed bed her, but this time be kind enough to leave the evidence. Wouldn't that salve the self-inflicted wound I carved with Frida? How nice to offset one dalliance with another. Tit for tat, and that's that. Instead of being forced to leave awkward calculations on the board. Rub them out, perhaps, but still their chalky residue remains.

Ramón was, of course, aware of the war in Europe, but he was flummoxed by the question presented him. He failed to see why the destruction of Europe should likewise mean the end of the painterly arts. If anything, he ventured, after wading lightly into the question's pool (lest there wait something unseen beneath the surface that might trip him up—a trap for him to negotiate in order to gain entrance to Trotsky's circle or be shut forever outside its gate) if anything, painting, and art in general, becomes more important in the wake of violent, indiscriminate destruction.

—Painting, of course, Trotsky said. Look to Picasso's *Guernica*. The carnage, the terror, the explosion of parts beneath the jagged threat of electric light. Though bombs are nowhere in it, it bespeaks the rising fascist militarism that even now is tugging at American bootstraps.

As Ramón made no comment, Trotsky twisted his goatee and continued.

—The United States' entry into the war, when it happens—and it *must* happen—will unleash a militaristic scourge upon this earth that will make the Nazis look like playactors. Hitler will be but John the Baptist to Roosevelt's— or, better, Uncle Sam's—fascistic messiah. Thus will history plunge into the final stage of capitalism. And it's all there, screaming from *Guernica*. But do tell me how some comely portrait of Trotsky—an exiled revolutionary, himself, to be sure—but how would his portrait pack any kind of revolutionary punch? It would, in fact, be wedded to the dead traditions of past centuries. Or, worse, to those monstrous worship portraits Stalin demands be painted of himself. And I will not knowingly set myself up to be idolized or daubed into the past, framed and nailed upon some wall.

—Yes, I think I understand, sir. But this is all immaterial. I have not, in fact, come to paint your portrait.

—Well I am not buying paintings, either, the Old Man assured him. The finances of this house are extremely tight at present, he considered adding. But he thought better of it before the revealing words could slip past his lips.

—Nor am I selling, the painter said, chuckling a bit. He drew his two canvases from their bundle to show the old Bolshevik. You see? Nothing, he smiled. I haven't painted a thing on them.

—Yes, I see that, Trotsky sighed. So what is it then?

The painter was confused.

—What is it you want?

—Ah, yes, the painter laughed, his chuckle dancing over the hearty thrust of exasperated air shot from the Old Man's nostrils. Your rabbits. I wondered if I might have a look at your rabbits.

—To paint them?

—No, said Ramón, struck once more by perplexity.

The Old Man remained silent. The heat of fear flickered at the base of his neck, but it quickly dissipated. The reality of the situation was that Trotsky did not feel frightened by his awkward guest, even if caution dictated that he should. The silence had ticked off a, by now, Pavlovian secretion of adrenaline to ignite the fight-or-flight response. But the Old Man's better sense caught this initial zap and wrestled it quickly into submission. The painter was, by all appearances, harmless. And Trotsky need only inquire further into the painter's desire to observe the rabbits to make solid sense of it. For example, he might start by asking, Are you an animal enthusiast? And then the painter might willingly divulge the keen interest he had taken in rodents since the time he'd been able to stand steadily on two legs and chase after them. Instead, for some reason, Trotsky said to the painter —The garden isn't much to look at, I'm afraid. In saying this, he turned to the scrub of lawn, cacti and short hedgerows with a sweep of his arm and thereby (foolishly, he would later admit) exposed a goodly portion of his back to this young stranger at his gate.

—I'm simply intrigued by the fact you keep them, the painter said. Imagine, the former War Commissar and Commander-in-Chief of the Red Army now shepherding a flock of rabbits.

—And chickens, Trotsky added, with a zeal he immediately regretted. But he sighed and tried not to dwell on the embarrassing gaffe. Well, he said finally in a defeated tone, let's have a look at them, then, shall we?

B became aware of me through an UNAM sociology professor I had contacted when first hunting for information on Tristessa/Esperanza. The professor led a class that examined society through the lens of literature and included readings of Burroughs' *Queer* and Kerouac's *Tristessa*, the latter translated into Spanish by Jorge García-Robles, who also wrote two informative books on Burroughs and Kerouac and their adventures in Mexico called *La bala perdida* and *La disfraz de la inocencia*, respectively. His Kerouac book contains the most detailed look at Villanueva that I know of, though, again, it primarily confines itself to the time when Esperanza was with Jack. Unfortunately, I have been unable to reach García-Robles to pan for additional material. If such even exists, which I highly doubt at this point. B is not coming.

It was another predictably gorgeous morning in Cuernavaca. But Fromm was not at all feeling himself. Looking out through the glass doors that opened onto the small patio, he marveled at the clear, static warmth of light that held the surrounding firs in a super exposure of greenness. He'd looked upon the trees at this hour of morning any number of times, but only now did the scene strike him as obscenely concrete and perfect. He frowned over the calm beauty, thinking that perhaps this was the perfect stillness that Suzuki was pointing him toward. But would it not be perfect boredom instead? Strange that this hadn't occurred to him before. Stranger still that he now found himself wondering if cigars would be allowed in the great communion with unconsciousness. Suzuki's sing-song voice filtered through this thought like the dust particles suddenly dancing in the screen of descending light outside.

—When the swordsman addresses his opponent, Suzuki was saying, he shouldn't think about the opponent, nor about himself, nor about the movements of his enemy's sword. He should simply be there with his sword, which, forgetting all technique, is ready to follow only the dictates of the unconscious.

Fromm noticed heads in front of him nodding. The rounded crests of trimmed hair bobbed like those of a group of surfacing and submerging breaststrokers. It made the psychologist sleepy. He blinked in rhythm with the nodding heads, his eyelids disturbingly heavy. He sat up and shook himself out of the stupor, and then lit a cigarette.

Suzuki was now presenting the example he had lifted from Kurosawa's *Seven Samurai*. Fromm had heard it before. The scene involved a test given individually to three samurai to see if they were up to the task of protecting the farmers' village. A youth hid inside the entrance to a building with directions from the test's administrator to strike each samurai with a pole as he entered. The first samurai was completely surprised and received the blow with full force. He failed the test, obviously. The second samurai went in, avoided the blow and took down his assailant. But he also was judged to have performed too poorly to pass the test. The third samurai stopped before entering the building and called out to whoever was inside, warning him that he should not try to attack a warrior experienced as he. This samurai alone was deemed capable of performing the job at hand since he had demonstrated the ability to sense danger without ever seeing it.

It was then (or, rather, at some point in the future separated by a passage of time in which Fromm sat smoking, wondering freely about the invisible enemies from his past, present and future—Suzuki was now asking about the nature of the unconscious, a question that would lead him to consider, in passing, the possibility of telepathy, before delving into the concept of *I*, recognizing that in discovering oneself—the movement of Zen—a person must follow a path in direct opposition to science, which is interested in the objective animalism of human beings, not in their humanity, not in the I; —I fear, Suzuki would warn, that men or women who don't aspire to knowledge of self should go through another cycle of birth and death) it was at that point that Fromm saw her. She was standing in the rear of the room near the open door to the hall, wearing thick, clear-framed sunglasses with square lenses. She had a thin oval face and her hair was pulled back in the traditional, circular braids of the Aztec. Perhaps she had come in with a message for somebody, Fromm thought. She wasn't one of the registered conference attendees, that much he was sure of. They had all arrived on time and been accounted for. Maybe she had simply seen the notice posted in the window to the street and wandered in thinking the event was free and open to the public. At the first break, he'd get up and kindly explain the situation to her. There was no hurry. She hardly looked the type set on causing a disturbance. If anything, she struck him as unnaturally silent and frail, almost vaporous.

She stood there expressionless, swaying at times in a rather frightening manner, as if she might faint and collapse at any moment. But even through these bouts of sick, careening motion, neither her features nor any other part of her body registered the slightest awareness of her condition. If she were to fall over, Fromm thought, she would go straight to the floor without extending an arm to brace herself.

Fromm continued watching her, finishing his cigarette as he did so. It left a tart, reedy flavor in his mouth. And the strange woman at the back of the room swayed now to a warm, waltzing clarinet that bubbled up from Fromm's nicotine-fueled memory. The melody was joined soon by an easy swing beat that felt frustratingly familiar to Fromm, though he was unable to place the song or the musicians playing it. Benny Goodman, he thought at first. But, no, the clarinet was too relaxed to be Goodman's. The song was a highly intimate number, not one of those that fired your pulse and pounded you into submission. (Although a brash trumpet at times did rise up and try to make it that.) Fromm returned to the clarinet, allowing it to play through its measures then fade just as the skipping piano came in. At that point, Fromm lifted the needle and returned it to the spot where the clarinet began its comforting tones. He let it play through to the piano again, then once more went back to the beginning. Soon the clarinet melody was happily looping in his mind and Fromm sat smiling sleepily. He even let his eyes close from time to time, allowing himself to drop deeper into the space of the music. But after one of the longer of these spells nodding off, he opened his eyes to find that the music had ceased and that the room was now painted with a new, intensely white light that vibrantly offset each of the room's angles, lines and curves.

—I referred earlier, Suzuki said, to the recent book by De Rougemont, *Man's Western Quest*, in which he names "the person" and "the machine" as two of the traits that distinguish the nature of the Western investigation of reality.

The woman at the rear of the room removed her sunglasses and rubbed her eyes with her left hand. Then she leaned back against the wall and Fromm observed her release a sigh (this action understood strictly through visual cues, which generated in his mind the corresponding sound of tired exhalation, though he did not actually hear it). The woman yawned and with it Fromm sat bolt upright. Dear God! It was Billie Holiday! Her sleepy eyes were cradled by disturbingly dark circles, as if she hadn't slept in several days but rather spent the time wallowing in some Mexican drug den. Nevertheless, there was no mistaking the singer. It was … yes … or maybe …

Suzuki was no longer speaking. He had stopped at some point back, Fromm suddenly realized, and was now looking at Fromm with a mixture of bemused and concerned curiosity. Though he couldn't recall doing so, Fromm assumed that he had gasped or otherwise remarked upon seeing Billie Holiday standing at the rear of the room (possibly he'd unknowingly supplied the audio missing from her visual sigh), and his reaction must have been strong (or strange) enough even to cut through the cat-like focus of the Zen master at his elbow. He offered Suzuki an impish grin, apologized and bid him continue.

—Well, the Western approach to life *is* rather shocking, the Buddhist quipped to excuse Fromm's audible gasp of surprise. Then he eased back into his speech as if it had but rolled on a little ways without him and he needed only to skip forward a touch to rejoin its path forward.

Fromm lit another cigarette and reclined in his seat next to Suzuki at the head table. He decided to hold off a bit before chancing another look at the woman in the rear of the room. First he would prepare himself, screening the image of her face in the safety of his mind, recalling and studying it there to the best of his abilities, inspecting each detail in the hope of confirming or rejecting his original impression without needing to face the eyes of the genuine article. But, of course, it could not be Billie Holiday. She was on tour somewhere, no doubt, and Mexico was hardly a hotbed for jazz, especially for the biggest names in the music. Although he did seem to recall reading somewhere (where in the world could that have been?) that Holiday was, at present, not in very good health. A sabbatical in some tropical locale—say, Cuernavaca, Mexico?—might not be completely out of the question. But still … a conference on Buddhism and psychoanalysis? Billie Holiday certainly would not …

And, indeed, she was not. When Fromm looked back, the woman, whether Billie Holiday or not, was no longer standing against the wall in the rear of the room. Nor could she be seen occupying any other part of it.

Wednesday morning found me once again on the patio (the smoking porch, that is) of El Globo pastry shop at the corner of Jalapa and Tabasco, washing down a banderilla and a concha de chocolate with a café americano, reading García-Robles' book on Burroughs, trying to determine a beneficial course of action for the day, action that might result in some unforeseen nugget of discovery that would further justify my impulsive trip to Mexico City. On the utility pole at the corner was posted an advertisement for a Thursday night lecture across the street at the Centro Budista. "The Relevance of Buddhism Today" was the talk's title. I jotted down the time of the lecture in my notebook, but knew even as I wrote that I wouldn't be attending. The truth is, I was exhausted. My feet ached and were badly blistered from walking around the city more than planned over the course of the preceding days (always in big cities I end up walking around much more than I had planned). By going to the lecture I could possibly gain some unique insight into the practice of Buddhism in modern-day Mexico and then trace that back to the days of Fromm and Suzuki. But such an exercise also struck me as merely a delay tactic—a way to justify not working, not conducting true research, through the hope that by simply living, reading, attending lectures, the necessary information would naturally reveal itself, links would snap together in my mind and my story would complete itself. Nevertheless, I was here. I should do *something*, even if its value wasn't readily apparent to me. What harm would there be in going to the lecture instead of hanging out in my hotel room watching TV?

But would I even understand the talk? That was another question. The Spanish, no doubt, would be way over my head, and I'd be sitting there dumb, struggling, a serious confidence sketched on my face, nodding occasionally to show all concerned that I was, indeed, getting it all, and, further, that I was a serious, understanding, contemplative and studious man—one to be noticed and admired—but really only catching about 20% of the words and even those dropping into my ears one by one as individual pebbles of disconnected vocabulary. The speaker would call on me then and invite me into some kind of participatory exercise that I'd be too proud not to enter, still faking, smiling stupidly, madly flushing, croaking a jumble of Spanish raked from a pile of tenses and conjugations—something that might be translated as "me they come looking for thoughts and I believe that maybe to learn what is the mode of Buddhism now in Mexico." The instructor would acknowledge this little piece of buffoonery with a warm chuckle and welcome me again with another lyrical stream of incomprehensible Spanish, to which I'd respond, Sí.

So, no, probably I would not go.

But what to do with *this* day? Or the morning even? It occurred to me after some mulling (and further reading on Burroughs and his antics in Mexico City) that I could retrace the steps Kerouac took that night in the rain running back from Esperanza's house in La Lagunilla, down past Garibaldi on Lázaro Cárdenas, through San Juan de Letrán and over into Roma Norte, down calle Orizaba to his rooftop abode above the apartment building at 210, where the junkie Bill Garver lived in an apartment that had previously housed the aforementioned Burroughs. It was a trip I had contemplated some weeks back, but had since forgotten in the anxiety of travelling and the pressing need to accomplish solid, documentable research. But now the idea of the walk came back to me in a pleasant, cleansing rush. Such an exercise would certainly kill the morning, and my feet should be able to tolerate it without too much further damage. I couldn't say exactly what I hoped to learn from such a trip, but it struck me as a piece of gumshoe research legitimate enough to curb (if, indeed, I was to take up the little jaunt) those feelings of deficiency that even the bright sun and cool Mexican air couldn't relieve me of—feelings that I wasn't accomplishing nearly enough here, that time was slipping away as I sat around at café tables or on park benches learning nothing new about Esperanza Villanueva, Jack Kerouac, Bill Burroughs, Leon Trotsky, Erich Fromm or anyone else who was elbowing for room in my story. The more I thought about it, finishing off my pastry at El Globo, the more expansive became the feeling that following Kerouac's footsteps was, indeed, not only a credible assignment, but one that could well yield beneficial, if perhaps indefinable, results. I was here, and shouldn't pass up an opportunity for discovery that I couldn't get anywhere else. So that was it. I closed the García-Robles book before I could begin to question myself anew, stuffed the volume into my backpack and brushed the remaining pastry crumbs from the table.

I caught the metro at Insurgentes and rode it east to Salto del Agua, where I got off and surfaced at the busy corner of José María Izazaga and Lázaro Cárdenas, where above the plaid streaming of people and cars loomed the massive brown edifice of Hotel Virreyes. Now spotted with age and serving as a hostel, it had, in its prime, in the 1950s, been a stop for movie stars, boxers and other assorted celebrities. Or so I had read somewhere. Needing to gain my bearings, I sat down on the edge of the cement planter running the length of the sidewalk and drew the Mexico City Guía Roji map book out from my backpack as clandestinely as possible. With north quickly situated, I returned the map book to my backpack and headed in the northerly direction up Cárdenas, planning to traipse the seven or eight blocks to the Torre Latinoamericana (constructed in 1956, a year after Jack's walk down this street) then turn back and retrace my steps to Izazaga and from there head west on what, according to the Guía Roji, was at that point called Arcos de Belén, running for a handful of blocks west to Niños Héroes, where it subsequently changed into Avenida Chapultepec (the way there, as I was to discover, lined with a toothing of structures erupted from the preceding decades—the stone and brick colonial places Jack would have passed squatting down between the rising, glass-heavy buildings of more recent modernity). Cárdenas is a commercial street, lined with stores selling clothes, shoes, electronics, fragrances, books, sporting goods. On the weekends the sidewalks are a pulsing mass of humanity. But in the middle of the week, on that Wednesday, there was room to walk freely, especially after I climbed the few steps rising from the sidewalk and rattled my way over the air grates laid close to the street above the metro line. The Torre Latinoamericana, a dirty, faded blue-green structure that looked hopelessly outdated from a distance—like a rickety vision of the future as seen in a 1950s sci-fi flick, stacked up on a miniature set for stop-action space creatures to crush and set aflame—gained nothing in architectural (or mythical) integrity as I drew nearer to it. At any minute, a strong wind might kick up and punch holes into the tower's shabby paper covering or blow it into a thousand erector set pieces. Deflated, I turned back when I was still several blocks away from the thing. The tower, and the street as a whole, was proving a poor cure for my traveler's depression. Not only was it failing to regurgitate the past as I had stupidly hoped, it wasn't even sparking me with a jolt of modern city *go*. The shops surely had not been here when Jack, numb on morphine and booze, his belly newly filled with a mess of gristly tacos, legged it home through torrents of rain in the dark gut of night. No, he didn't pass shops like this: vendors of all manner of mass-produced wares, stuffed onto shelves that reached to the ceiling or onto racks that overpopulated the showroom floor, the nondescript buildings pressing one into the next for a depressing brown mile. Back at the Izazaga and Cárdenas intersection, I turned right, moving west past that mix of modern and colonial buildings earlier mentioned. Jack instead writes of "that last series of bars that end in a ruined mist, fields of broken adobe, no bums hidden, all wood, Gorky, Dank, with sewers and puddles, ditches in the street five feet deep with water in the bottom—powdery tenements against the light of the nearby city." I passed over Niños Héroes and continued on Avenida Chapultepec till the sidewalk terminated in a cement triangle in the center of a busy intersection. A vagrant with a ragged goatee reclined against a monument to Dr. Eduardo Liceaga, an important medical and cultural figure from turn-of-the-twentieth-century Mexico, who, among other accomplishments, had helped design and bring into being Mexico City's General Hospital. The good doctor stood in stone atop this ignored monument, stranded, as I was, on that patch of cement stretching as an isthmus into the rush of multilane traffic. I backtracked a bit and after waiting an agitated minute found a large enough break in the flow of traffic to cross over to Dr. Río de la Loza, where, heading west again, I was happy to discover that the fat road running north/south past Dr. Liceaga's triangle was indeed Avenida Cuauhtémoc, which was on my planned route. I took Cuauhtémoc south with something of a renewed skip in my step. But the vigor proved short-lived. After only a few short blocks, I was surrendering to the benches in the Jardín Dr. Ignacio Chávez, as my knees and feet were aching terribly and perspiration was freely draining from my forehead. I chose a bench next to an elderly couple who took turns holding a red, leather leash hooked to a gray terrier that, in any event, sat at the old man's feet without moving. A couple in their twenties sat several benches away, allowing their large, chocolate-colored mutt—maybe a lab-pinscher mix?—to run freely about, his barks echoing off nearby buildings. As could have been expected, the mutt was soon at the terrier, and his young, male owner ran over to separate the two and keep his dog from eating the terrier and/or the elderly couple. Besides the loud, repeated cracks of barking, no harm was done, and with the animals separated (the mutt off to retrieve a tennis ball tossed by its owner deep into the park), the couples exchanged pleasantries, asked on the age, health, etc. of each other's pet and generally breezed over the earlier incident. Everyone in Mexico City has at least one dog, so the barking and antics in the parks and on the sidewalks are tolerated as openly as the inevitable mayhem of playing children. I got up from my bench and moved on.

I crossed over Cuauhtémoc, then cut through the Jardín Pushkin to head west on Alvaro Obregón. The Cine México, the post office, the Cine Balmori were no longer there as they had been in Jack's day. Now there were the many chic (and not so chic) restaurants, bars, hotels, cafés. La Perla de Oriente (now Los Bisquets Bisquets Obregón), which opened its doors in 1945, would have been there for Jack, though undoubtedly closed at 2 a.m. when he passed that way, and he doesn't mention it. He continued, as I did, to Orizaba, where we turned left and rattled two blocks—I dry, but with aching joints and bones; Jack's head and feet soaked, but feeling no pain (or anything else) owing to the erasure effect of the morphine—to Plaza Luis Cabrera, where the fountain was dead for Kerouac, but sprayed sonorous, comforting arches for me into the blue, late-morning Wednesday. I stopped and sat on an iron bench on the sunny eastern side of the fountain. I sat there for a long time, I don't know how long, simply watching the water spray and allowing its vibrant, white noise to fill my empty head and shower down into my dispirited back and chest. Jack would run farther down the street to his place at Orizaba 210. But I decided I'd had enough. If I was throwing away a unique chance for discovery in Mexico City, so be it. I was through. After about twenty minutes I got up and went into my hotel there on the eastern side of the plaza.

—We're going dancing, Monica said.

—We are?

She nodded and took my hand, guiding me in wind-whipping fashion through the stone, canyon streets of old silver town Guanajuato. Leaning forward to drag me, her straight black hair stretching out like racing lines as she looked back, struggling with mock grimace.

Or she walked slowly, rather, barely glancing back to check that I was following. I thought several times of ducking quietly into some shop or pool hall. Ditch her. But I didn't.

—We're going dancing, she said sternly. You and me. Come on.

—Come on, we're going dancing.

—Do you like dancing?

—Are you American?

—I don't, I said, or should have.

—Americans are so boring, she might have said. You just need to live. Let your hair down.

Black lengths of hair encircling my neck as we danced. Michael Jackson, perhaps. And she pushed back, playfully twitching her index finger back and forth at me. No, no, no. Hips swaying away in retreat.

—What do you do in America? as we meandered over enclosed, cobbled streets toward the club, the night air warm with the scent of eucalyptus trees.

I ordered a cognac after downing the two beers that were included in the price of the cover charge.

Then it was bright the next day waking up on the cell's cement bench.

—I write.

—For magazines and stuff?

—Books. Crime fiction, mostly. Some erotica.

No, I didn't say that. That last part about the smut. What would her reaction have been? Where would the night have led differently? Would it have ended right there? In which case I should have said it.

—I *specialize* in porn, actually.

—Are you, how do you say, a whacker?

—Wanker. Yes, certainly, every chance I get.

—Does it pay much?

—No, it's just a hobby, you know.

—The writing, I mean.

—Oh, of course, the writing. Yes, loads. I'm filthy rich.

She nodded, not certain about any of it. But in a different country, who knows what's possible.

Only she never heard those things, so she didn't have to decide about them.

—Crime fiction is a bit silly, I think.

—Of course it is, I said. Most of it. But that's what the people want. That and science fiction. Which is silly too, more often than not—porn for those who demand scientific fact in every other facet of their lives.

—Your detective writing is not silly then? Yours is different?

—Sometimes it is, sometimes it isn't. But writing is always silly to some degree, I imagine, no matter its type.

Again she was uncertain, although her dubiousness cut across all territorial and linguistic lines. Detective stories were crap in any language, in any land.

—At times I have ambition to push beyond procedurals and produce something more complex, more unpredictable, more meaningful, I guess.

—More meaningful, she repeated, whether to understand the phrase or question its validity, I wasn't certain.

—I've mostly given up on that, though, I assured her.

The 30-peso cover charge got you into the club with two beer tickets. All the beer was gone within an hour, so you were forced then to empty your wallet for more expensive fare (or go without, which really wasn't an option). Except for the college kids who ran out to the local liquor store and brought back bottles to share amongst themselves (with no interference from the club owners) or sell off in Dixie cups or mixed with glasses of Coca-Cola to less resourceful patrons.

—And where else does it hurt? the doctor asked, after inspecting my eyes, my nose and pressing his thumbs to my forehead. Algún dolor más?

—Aquí, I said, placing my hand on my left hip.

Perhaps he wasn't a doctor. There was no way of knowing.

She seemed hesitant to tell me about herself. Where she came from, what she did for a living, a sampling of her hopes and desires. All were brushed aside with great skill and inviting laughter.

—We need to dance.

But there were curious lapses in her deflections. Little holes she carelessly allowed to puncture her tough, swinging skin.

—This is how we used to do it in Carrizo Springs! hollered while dancing.

—You haven't had your belly warmed till you drink some Lagunilla punch! later while drinking rum and Coke.

—Sex is so not worth it for love, grumbled at some point.

I stopped at the corner, pressing my back against the building's stone façade, the right edge of my body stroked in a fine line of blue light. I looked back. But the road snaked steeply up the hill into close, pressing darkness. I heard nothing. Or, rather, I heard all manner of things, the most minute insect clatter, expanding to populate the tonal web with a sonorous cluster that effectively blocked the interjection of any critical, giveaway noises—footsteps, voices, the rattle of a trash can lid skipping off the stone street. I moved on. Went deeper into the spiraling city, sucked farther away from light with every advancing step. They were, perhaps, chasing me there, never wanting to catch me at all, but simply out to flush me into the void. And I went. Unable to do otherwise. Not wanting to do otherwise. Drawn to this undoing, to this oblivion—physically craving it, while horribly frightened. So I went, on and on. Drinking in the sickening strong, blood-warm punch of self-demise. My temples pounded with it. Come and take me! I cried. But, later … No, don't. Go away! I want to be alone!

—You'll have to pay for that, she said, removing my hand from her hip.

I asked her how much it would cost, but she only grinned.

—I've forgotten, she said coyly, or might have, pressing her finger into her chin, tilting her head sharply to the right and rolling her eyes up into mock thought. Gee, she said.

—Golly, and I stroked the back of her neck.

—Shazam! she punched me in the gut. Playfully, though.

But there I lay, crumpled on the pavement, life waning from me with a pinched nasally whistle and tin-can echo in the underpass. There in the gutter, where flowed blood and urine. There where my belt cuffed my arms behind my back. There were I moaned. There where I howled. There where I fainted and came to again and again. There where you left me. There where they collected me. There from whence they took me and put me away. There where I cried. And spoke your name. And promised to follow you. Wishing I'd obeyed you. Or listened to you, some, even a little. Wishing I had thought. Before acting. If ever the two can be separated in such a way.

Or is everything going always, always going. Into a wall, into a hook, into a descending tire iron. Which is where they pick you up and drag you away and lay you out for dead or waking.

This time I woke.

—You were drunk, the policeman said.

—Fui robado. Even at that moment, with my face throbbing, I was instantly concerned about my Spanish grammar, worried I had spoken incorrectly, or, at least, somewhat less than perfectly. Still the message seemed to register on my interrogator's face.

—Tienes que responder a algunas preguntas.

Of course I would. Always more questions to answer. More accusations to deflect. Which made me burn, even though the inquiries were not without their justification. After all, I went rather willingly into the darkness. Into the grinding blackout. Even if it was rather impossible for me to do otherwise. Even if my interrogators were the same ones, possibly, who took me down.

—You will need to pay a fee in order to leave, said a translator brought in by the guard to explain my situation to me.

—The only money I have is back at my hotel.

—And which hotel is that?

—I can't remember.

The translator was suspicious.

—Its name begins with an M. That's all I can remember.

The translator nodded, though he still appeared less than satisfied. Next, a lawyer of some sort came in with a clipboard and asked me to explain everything that had happened the previous night. I explained it to her the best I could, inventing things (or at least not questioning the foggy images that popped into my head) in order to fill any gaps.

—They struck me over the head with some kind of pipe, I concluded, and left me lying in the gutter of an underpass as their car sped away. All of this spoken, to some degree or other, in Spanish. Perhaps the story came out quite different than intended.

—Te habían secuestrado en el carro?

—No entiendo. But I did understand, more or less. And having been held in the back of the car by my attackers was, indeed, one version of the movie that played out in my head. In that one, another car pulled up behind us as we went into the underpass. Both cars stopped and we all got out. In another version I was walking along the sidewalk in the underpass when both cars pulled up. In a third, there were no cars involved and the underpass was much smaller and darker and there was only one assailant. Another take had me in an empty plaza surrounded by a gang and an old indigenous woman pushing a cart. No entiendo. It was a convenient way not to decide on a story.

The lawyer nodded and wrote something on her clipboard. Vale, she said, regresaré. And, indeed, she did return, more than once, asking essentially the same questions each time and noting my responses again and again on her clipboard.

The doctor came later, reached through the prison bars and pressed his thumbs into my forehead.

—I bet I could hurt you, Monica said, grinning. Yes, it would be easy.

—Not so easy, I don't think.

—Yes, I think so.

—Have you been searching for a girl like me? she asked at some other point in the evening.

—Not particularly.

—I've been searching for someone like you. Do you believe me?

—No. I didn't believe her, but the effect was rather the same. I imagined that she had, indeed, been looking for me and, through the pleasantly suffocating cloud suddenly enveloping my brain, I asked her why.

—You're a fool.

No, I'm not sure she said that. I don't remember what she said. Maybe none of it was said. I was free to go, however. That was a relief. As they returned my shoes and belt, I again protested that I had been robbed and that the cops should be looking into the real crime, the real criminals, instead of locking me away for a night. But nobody was much in the mood. And I thought it best then just to move on. Locate my hotel, collect my things, get home and rest. Rest, most of all. Rest for a good long time till it was all somewhat better.

—Tomorrow we may die, Monica said to me. So we are nothing.

—That's exactly right, I agreed, spinning her some on the dance floor. You're exactly right.

The red lights over the dance floor shifted, casting stretched, gyrating shadows onto the club's milky basement walls.

—And I'm *seek*, she grinned, tossing her head back while being spun. Terribly, terribly *seeeeeek*.

I woke in a drugged daze. Such was the turmoil of those days that I needed to ingest a sedative before retiring to bed each evening. So I came to slowly, figuring through the weight of the fog that the locals were celebrating yet another of their Mexican holidays, banging off fireworks into the pit of night. But the shots grew steadily closer, descending through the night, through the trees, through the roof, till they were exploding in rapid succession directly above my head, with the acrid scent of gunpowder burning into my nostrils. Natalia was on top of me and both of us were on the floor behind the bed. The gunfire sprayed into the walls. Bullets, plaster and glass ricocheted and fell about the room.

—Move, I whispered to Natalia, and it somehow cut through the chaotic racket in a clear, pointed directive. Next, she slid from me and lay flat on the floor at my side. Where was everyone?! It was one of those dreams that I drugged myself to avoid, wherein the entire guard detail and the group of policemen who lived on the premises had, through a series of unforeseen and most improbable events, left the house open for easy attack, drifting away to a variety of tasks requiring their immediate attention at the least fortuitous of moments, thereby allowing a stream of approaching assassins to pour into the compound and riddle my body with bullets from every imaginable angle.

And Seva! Where was the boy? We had brought him here a month earlier only to be sliced to shreds in his bed. He may have awoken just in time to feel the metal rip into his body. He is dead now. I moved to get up, but Natalia's hand pressed on my chest, holding me back. Bullets traced a quick web of metal death above us. It was hopeless. Seva was only the first. We were all dead. The attack had finally come. Stalin's farmhands had, at last, torn up the few remaining crops amidst its expanding field of riotous weeds.

And it was in that moment, lying flat on my back looking up at the cutting net of mortality, that I decided to escape.

Later, stumbling, careening blindly along the banks of the river Churubusco and then up through the dark blue streets of Colonia Del Valle, the stinging divide from self ignited my head into a crazy sprouting of tender, green stems that rose into a twisted piling of stimulated antennae, ever growing. Back in the house on the calle Vienna I still lay dying, or was already dead, or was crying over Natalia or Seva, cupping my hands over their flowing wounds. *That* Trotsky, if he had survived, would get up and go on to the rest of the life that awaited him. And perhaps I should be there with him, accepting that fate, making it whole, one way or the other, for better or for worse. But it was too late for such misgivings now. I had fled. Cut and run with a horrifically numb finality. And yet, somewhere in the gut of this cold, hollow carcass that chugged with aching thighs up la calle Patricio Sanz, there rattled the dread certainty (even as I tried to suppress it as but another gastrointestinal disturbance) that I would forever be catching myself up in the lines of this other man that I had left, lines that with a wild, tumbling certainty had already etched themselves into the ledger of accountable glass. My breath would cloud as his breath, and lift and shudder and foul the human air as his might.

I would trip on his pronouncements, his thoughts and calculated violence. Still, this new manufacturing of myself (be it the shimmering core climbed from the rubble or the slimy coward leapt free of the spray of martyrdom) continued running, headlong now up the calle Fresa and spilling into the Parque San Lorenzo, where the basketball courts were empty and the quiet fountain sat by in a cold display of its iron indifference to transformation. And there, finally, I sat, submitting my weakened back to the upright torture of an iron bench, hoping against all sense that the hour might graciously fall in and bury me in its collapse.

I am reading Fromm's essay "Psicoanálisis y Budismo Zen" on the way to Chalma. Zen: mix of Hindu rationality and abstraction with the sense of Chinese concreteness and realism. Psychoanalysis = a-religious, scientific method. Zen = religious, spiritual salvation; "illumination." Ahora, now, in the modern world, "being" is dominated by "having." We are living only to avoid insecurity and solitude. A man is let on the bus to check tickets and count heads. Tall office buildings blink alive from the hills on the outskirts of town. Ford. Ericcson. RBS. Movistar. Lomas Memorial. Ever construction on ever more buildings. Another man is let on to sell gelatinas, flanes, jugos con leche (de fresa y que más?). A few travelers ascend and join us as well. Freud's theory, according to Fromm, is one for "salvation." Fog over the pines on the hills leaving the city on highway. Housing structures built into the hills. CFE electric plant. Looping exit ramp for Chalma. Pick up one person in little stretch of town—line of buildings on either side of a muddy road and nothing else (like an Old West set on a Hollywood back lot, though this with candy-colored façades and no customers for the bins of fresh vegetables and fruits or for the fresh rubber tires stacked outside the open doors of auto repair shops). Later, round the bend, shelters with picnic tables scattered over acres of open, rolling grass fields, and race tracks for 4x4 all-terrain vehicles, fences with GOTCHA banners stretched over them, crumbling shops and restaurants lining the side of the road in failing stone and brick. Valle de Silencio announces a sign arching over a drive into one of these ATV picnic parks. One little brick castle sits off by itself, crumbling into history. Bienvenidos a la Valle de Conejo reads another sign near the spot where a dead horse lies stretched to its last by the side of the road. Those busy nearby with their chores pay no more attention to the dead beast than they would to a freshly formed puddle. Fresh construction of resaurante Los Pinos on the right side of the road. Corn fields. Two passengers who boarded at the edges of Mexico City now descend the steps and walk off into the middle of nowhere. A new building of plaster and glass—Nissan dealership—muy moderno, planted directly alongside broken-down shacks. In the middle of nowhere. These little pop-up towns all along the road. Statue of Benito Juárez (in granite?). Daimler factory. For Freud, man is a machine. Mansión Inn, with purple, pink and yellow arches. Now more cornfields—de veras—retreated in planted rows to the mountains in the distance. Small, black sheep in field of small town. Who buys this stuff (food, etc.) from all these roadside stores? A crippled (legless?) girl is hoisted into the back of a taxi by a pair of stout men. We pass a field of nopales. A man on a ten-speed bike rides the curvy, descending road. Por alguna razón, tengo menos (ningun?) miedo y ansiedad que antes. Fromm sounding very religious now (p. 96): "El fin de la vida es nacer plenamente, aunque su tragedia es que la mayoría de nosotros muere antes de haber nacido asi." Several cyclists descend in front of the bus, along with a pickup carrying a large crucifix tied up over a display of flowers in the truck bed. Two young men sit alongside the cross as escorts. Corn on the side of the hill. Sharply winding road descending. Brightly colored restaurants crowd street sloping into Chalma. Yes? No. Ya no es Chalma. Es otra lugar. We roll on. Roadside shop on turn with many large (3 ft.?) wood crucifixes for sale. Traffic slowing, compacting, wedging into slim streets with vendors' stalls on either side. Colored plastic tarps stretch over tables of wares, trinkets, snacks, musical instruments, various items of Catholic iconography. The bus bogs down in merging lines of traffic. The man across the aisle from me gets up and says a few words to the driver. The door opens and the rider descends. We move forward a couple feet. Two more riders get off. Now a fourth. The driver adds his blaring horn to the cacophony of perturbed drivers. After conferring with one another, the elderly couple in the front seat also kindly ask permission to leave the bus. The door opens. We inch forward. Stop again at the curve where the street plunges through the heart of town. The final three riders get up and give their thanks to the driver. There is only me, now, with the driver, and I stick it out, riding down through town where the crush of traffic eases and we coast down to the bus station. A couple of vendors silently offering crowns fashioned from tiny flowers greet the stopped bus and are disappointed to find that only a sole rider—yo—remains. They express their displeasure to the driver, who lifts his shoulders, explaining that the others had departed in town. I use the restroom in the small bus station, then buy a Coke and some Japanese peanuts from the station's snack shop. I ask the man working there how to get to the church. To the right, and up the hill, he says. Of course. Just like in Dante. I go. Through the tightly hugging vendor stalls, where all manner of merchandise is up for grabs: clothing, food, CDs, religious items. I walk, uncertain that I am actually heading toward the church, as side streets branch off here and there. But I stick with the crowd. At a certain point I exit into a small park of sorts, its circular, stone-paved courtyard supporting a stone cross at its center. From the cross (or perhaps it's better to say *to* the cross) runs an aqueduct siphoning the water from the river up the hill. The aqueduct also empties into a large stone pool a few steps up from the courtyard, where children and some other travellers wade, play and bathe, hoping, I imagine, to soak up the supposed holy properties of the water hereabouts. I walk up the steps to get a better view from the top of the hill. A young couple approaches me. The man, probably in his early twenties, hoists a small plastic bag in his left hand to show me the bundled weight at its bottom. Amigo, he says, beginning to smile, quieres comprar mi corazón? Or perhaps he says un corazón or even otro corazón. The woman with him begins to laugh and he soon joins her. I laugh too and tell him no thanks. We are a warm trinity of jokesters. Then I go down and rejoin the dark, crowded path that descends as a tunnel and empties, a hundred yards or so farther on, onto the courtyard of the church. Life-size plastic horses are set up outside for tourists to sit upon and have their pictures taken like real vaqueros just in from the hills. Inside the old church, the penitents, the faithful, the curious stuff in beneath the ornate golden columns and arches, the crystal white domes and the dark-skinned Christ hanging there above the altar. As I enter and sit to rest in a pew, a crowd of penitents are performing a certain ritual that has them now backing away from the altar in a slow, solemn, crowded procession, clutching large wooden crosses to their breasts. So it was here that Esperanza Villanueva came with her husband Dave Tesorero to try and cure themselves of addiction, or at least scrub themselves of the sin of it. And where Tesorero and Burroughs came, earlier one would imagine, to sell heroin on the down-low at the side altar of la Virgen de Dolores. I snake with the rest of the crowd to the left of the main altar and leave the sanctuary, go into an antechamber where I avoid the ridiculous tumult of holy water being flicked down upon the faithful from the wands of old, bent priests, turn down a steep tunneling of steps to a chapel that houses a bloodied, dejected Christ lounging on a chair above an altar, his head cradled in his right hand, a long staff propped, defeated, in his left. Below him on the altar is an oblong glass box with heavy wood trim. It holds two skulls and a smattering of other bones. I go back up the stairs out of the crypt and turn out of the church into the glowing summer air, pass over the thick stone bridge that straddles the rushing river, and work my way back around to the front of the church and start back up through the tunnel of merchants that leads to the bus station. Only now, going back, do I notice that the Aztec Sun Stone is stamped, every few yards or so, into the cement of the market street. A man on his knees waddles down the street toward the church, stopping as I pass him and reaching down to adjust his kneepads. Also I notice the many heads flowered with crowns (those like I had refused from the vendors who approached my bus). I go back. And in the station, waiting for my return bus, snacking on chips, I watch a lame, sandy-colored dog cross the station floor, her teets thick and extruding down the length of her belly, left hind leg held off the ground, limping. She ascends a short series of stone steps. A male Dalmatian follows not too far behind, but when he gets too close he's called off tersely by a man sitting nearby reading a newspaper. A band of musicians marches past outside on the street, the tuba thumping hard and low beneath the sharp blare of trumpets, before the band slowly dissipates into the crush of vendors. I am going back again, the bus moving over the street more freely than when it had come in. But a young woman and two men emerge from a tarp-covered shop and wave the bus to a stop. The driver argues with them for a bit, apparently declining their request to board—refusing the terms they would like—then finally closes the door in their faces and moves on. On. Past all the squat houses and roadside shops, like the curiously named Miscelánea Mary that appears to deal mostly in roses. Later, at an intersection in a small town, school children board. They scurry happily to the back of the bus and thrust all the windows wide open, funneling strong winds into the cruising vehicle. The kids filter off at various locations, but the windows remain agape for the rest of the trip. The last student rides for an hour or better, disembarking at a faraway outcropping of houses that descends a steep hill and spreads out into the open valley below. It is his sad, daily commute, no doubt—morning and afternoon, for years. Buildings are being built every-where. By farmers? For them? So many structures left in some state of construction or destruction. Satellite dishes (SKY, VeTV) on nearly every cinderblock house. Back through the rolling hills of pine. Back through the open plains in the shadow of blue mountains where frail-looking houses slant against the elements, and kids play near the bodies of stripped-down automobiles. Back past the ATV parks with their wood fences and covered picnic tables. Once on the highway again, a state (or bus company?) official of some nature boards to check our tickets. He gets off a little later and a little later still, on the edge of the great city, some other officials board and check our tickets once more—an unnecessary doubling up of security, performed, it would seem, simply to give these men a free ride back into town. Back to the high-rise office towers. Back into traffic, into the jammed city, where cars and trucks scrape by each other at incredible speeds, and the construction continues on the highway and nearby buildings—always continues—as if beyond human control, the steel, cement, thick cable and glass rising from the earth to stretch over human activity as an octopus of smothering destruction. An ambulance tries to squeeze through the dense, belching foliage of afternoon traffic. An impossible venture. Yet it manages to pull it off somehow, disappearing into the crush of machinery as if none of it had ever existed.

Reflections of an Officer from the Investigation
into the Failed Trotsky Assassination

The floor was littered with .22 caliber cartridges. That's what I remember immediately, the copper glint from the spilled ammo reminding me for some reason, by some trip in memory, of the flapping orange wings of Monarch butterflies when they commandeer the forest floors a bit west of here—in the oyamel fir forests in the western part of the state of Mexico and into Michoacan. Have you ever seen that? Each year they come and populate the forest just before the Day of the Dead. The indigenous people have long believed that the migrating butterflies are the returning souls of dead children and warriors. Though now I hear the Monarchs and their migration are being endangered by climate change, by drought and wildfires in Texas. But there's also the human action: the widespread use of herbicides in fields of crops genetically modified to resist them. So the corn and soybeans keep growing, but the milkweed that the Monarchs depend on gets wiped out. And there's also problems with illegal logging in the Mexican forests themselves, depleting the acceptable area for the butterflies to land. So if the Monarchs one day stop coming, how will the indigenous myth change to account for the evaporation of all those lost souls?

The other thing that sticks in my mind about the first few minutes searching in that house for the remnants of Trotsky's would-be assassins was the empty artist's canvas set up on an easel in the center of the main room. Its whiteness, which was rather yellowed, actually, as I remember, seemed almost to cast a reflection as we worked inspecting the place. Several times I'd catch that block of canvas out of the corner of my eye and, startled, I'd turn expecting to find a mirror there. It had that effect. But, of course, it was only an annoying piece of stretched canvas. Still, later, I'd make the same mistake again. And then again. Ha! It was infuriating. Later we found an empty pack of Lucky Strikes lying around. I honestly don't remember who found it. It could've been me, even, but I don't think so. But that was a key for us, because it told us that an American had been there. And by American, you'll have to excuse me, I mean someone from the USA. For, yes, all of us in these two conjoined continents are Americans aren't we? Excuse me.

Anyway, the corpse, disturbingly, was copper too when we uncovered it. It'd been covered in quicklime when they buried him and the skin had become tinted. To this day there are certain shades of copper that awaken the stench of rotting flesh in my nostrils. And certain smells, like if I come across a dead animal, that cause me to see a brassy color and I automatically get a little sick. Even all these decades later that happens.

We were looking for David Alfaro Siqueiros, the painter, for, as you know, he was the leader of that band that made the hit on Trotsky's house in May

1940, in the middle of the night, a hit the Old Man and his wife and grandson all somehow miraculously survived. And, I don't remember all the particulars, but that led us to that adobe house out on la calle Desierto de los Leones. After poking around for quite a while in the ground-floor rooms, and not finding too much of anything, other than the .22 cartridges and the canvas and the Lucky Strike pack, we went down into the basement. There was a kitchen of sorts down there, and we recognized immediately that the dirt floor had been disturbed not too long before. Somebody—some guy living thereabouts, I think, who wasn't part of our team—dug up the spot with a pickax. I don't know why we didn't do it ourselves. Maybe we didn't have the tools, which seems kind of shortsighted now. But, nevertheless, this other guy volunteered or we persuaded him and he came over and started chipping away at the earth. Well, it didn't take him long. The body was only something like two feet down. And the smell hit us as soon as the first part of flesh was uncovered. It was instantly unbearable. So we called in the pros. Ha! Even with the little time I spent down there with that stench, it still haunts me. I—and everybody else too—wasn't staying down there once that smell hit. Hell no! So the forensic team came in and they got the body out. Two bullets in the head is how they did him, probably while he was sleeping. Poor bastard went to sleep and never woke up. I wonder sometimes if he expected it, knowing he shouldn't sleep, never intending to, but then his body simply giving way, betraying him and that's how he went out. Anyway, that's how I imagine it. A suicide of sorts—an automurder, if you will. Poor Bob, as Trotsky himself would later say, hearing about it. Poor Bob …

And what did Siqueiros do after that but enjoy success and international renown as one of Mexico's great muralists? Yeah, they held him for a while and there was a trial, but, as so often happens in Mexico, nothing much came of it. He had to leave the country for a few years, I think. But how many people who see Siqueiros' work now know anything about the role he played in trying to assassinate Trotsky? Or, if they do, how many treat it as anything other than just intriguing cocktail party chatter? And there was that other painter too. What was his name? Arenal. Luís Arenal and his brother were part of it, and probably the ones who actually killed Bob Harte. Amazing really. Fucking painters. Ha! But those were the times. Everything had that heightened sense of importance. Except life, perhaps, no?

—It's difficult, I whined to Leonard. What is there really left to write about?

—I hear ya, he grinned. But he'd rather not have been listening. Another lit patron to fawn over in order to keep the alcohol sales flowing. And Leonard, I gathered, even at his young age, was already long past the point of enjoying any of the buffoonery. He was operating on autopilot. People become so ridiculous and boring when they drink. Or they start out that way, which is why we drink to begin with—to make it all bearable and seemingly interesting, and then profound, then emotionally vital and, again, weepingly profound, sometimes worth slugging over, other times countered only by surrendering a forehead to the edge of the bar. Many other times you can simply laugh over it resignedly. Leonard would stand there and laugh with you and say Yes. Yes, I hear ya, man. Sure thing. It sucks. What can you do? Fucked up. Ridiculous. I know. Yes. If it's not one thing it's another. I've been there. Shit. Pure, unadulterated *mierda*. You know it? What can you say? Worthless. Howl. Wake the dead. It's over. Move on. Sit up. Take note. What for? You hear me? Unbelievable. Unbelievable.

Need another?

—The past is the present! Trotsky thundered into the telephone in the café in Pachuca. The barman looked up, but quickly lowered his chin again, returning to his work as if nothing peculiar had happened. Perhaps he wiped the bar more vigorously now. Trotsky tried to steady himself, and repeated meekly, resignedly, apologetically —The past is the present.

—Oh, Lvionochek, no. No. You have to move on from these things.

And though voiced as a sentiment toward reconciliation—a moving on together—his wife was already beginning to formulate the thoughts that would congeal in her mind the following day and find their way onto her stationery, forming a line that her husband, upon receiving the letter, would underline in red crayon, as if striking back against a pointed attack: Everyone is, in essence, terribly alone, she wrote.

And what waited for everyone at the end of the line was the grave.

But she didn't write that last line. Or say it, even. She was quiet.

Still Trotsky was moved to intone with an unsteady jaw —Vamos a vivir, Natasha. Vamos a vivir.

He might have added, No matter what. But he didn't add this.

—You have to be willing to go to bat at all hours, he grinned, the thick black mustache seeming to become fuller even as it stretched above his lips. And keep all the burners on the stove firing. That's really cooking! he laughed. That's a pro.

—But why put yourself through it at all?

—How do you mean?

—I mean what's the point?

—The point? Here the executive who bore a striking resemblance to Carlos Fuentes leaned forward and sat up, his astonishment awakening him to a heighted level of economic awareness. The point?! Well, Jesus, the point, to be blunt, is money!

He laughed nervously upon saying this, then ran a quick finger across his lips.

—You need money, don't you? he added, the release of breath alone relieving him of much of the financial agitation that had exercised him a moment earlier.

—Well, sure, Ramón granted. But only because we've created money as a system of exchange. It's now an accepted and deeply engrained fiction. But you don't need money like you need, say, water. Money is something we've chosen to rely on.

The businessman studied his inquisitor, this twentysomething interloper of true Mexican lineage who drank Anchor Steam and reclined into the evening hours with a nonchalance that bespoke a carelessly muddy future. Fuentes' fingers played again with his lips as if working to twist shut the flow of bemusement rippling his features, hoping he might check the mirth before it ran over into all-out chuckling.

—Okay, you have a point, he allowed the youth after gathering himself. If you want to get philosophical about it. But there are a whole lot of things we modern humans have come to rely on. Take yourself back to the Stone Age if you want (here he couldn't help but deposit a chuckle), but the rest of us are quite happy living here in the modern world. You want to sit out the game, be my guest. But badmouthing the rest of us for playing ... well, that just sounds like a lot of sour grapes.

—I'm not even against money, necessarily, Ramón continued. It's just that living your life merely to collect green paper seems a little bit silly to me.

—But you don't just think it's silly, a suddenly stoic Fuentes asserted. You're actually mad about it.

—I'm mad, or at least very dejected, because this game of yours has become so pervasive. People don't have a choice over whether or not they want to play it. In the end, participation is mandatory, isn't it? Even if that participation simply amounts to playing the forfeiting loser.

—Sour grapes, Fuentes grinned. Sour, fucking grapes.

He took a healthy swallow of his beer and let that latest pronouncement sink in.

—So tell me, he said then. What are you good at, Ramón?

—I paint.

—Hm hmn, the executive hummed through another mouthful of ale, pointing at the younger man as he lowered the pint glass to the bar. There, you see? Now what if instead of money we all traded in paintings? And those with the best paintings could trade them for the best consumer goods, would hold the highest status in society, have the best houses, etcetera. Now wouldn't you be for that?

—No. I can't say that I would be.

—Of course you would be!

Now Ramón was compelled to laugh.

—You can't break out of this mode of consumption, can you?

—Hey, we're consumptive animals. It's only natural.

—No, it's far from natural, I assure you.

—I'm a completely natural, virile, male human being. We make money. That's what we do.

—I see, Ramón said, shaking his head, a tired grin signaling his wish to bury the conversation. Well then, he said in conclusion, I suppose you can buy the next round for us.

I've taken to studying flies—my own entry into Zen, I guess—as they twitch across the wrinkled stones of Plaza Luis Cabrera, my brain, sitting hard and block-still atop my spinal column, buzzing shut to the pestering whisper of depression. Why have I come here? What did I hope to find? What, other than my own inability to produce, to discover, to live? But no, no questions that concrete present themselves. They will only come later, upon reflection. In the moment the brain is dead, stirred only by the occasional dull echo calling for action that lifts into the breeze then quickly surrenders itself to the sparkling drone of the raining fountain. It is gone now. Here the brain sits dead like rock, content to watch and not understand, not even try to understand. Just watch.

Because comprehension is beyond me, and I've run out of places to walk and my feet are as tired as my brain and just as ripe with blisters. Yet still I get up from time to time to spiral around Colonia Roma looking for a satisfactory café to sit and rest my feet and occupy myself with coffee. But most of the places have already had their fill of me, accepting me with wary, annoyed eyes and giggles on the lips, followed by sighs of exasperation—I can go to a place maybe twice before feeling unwelcome. Though the feeling, no doubt, is wholly self-generated, speaking more to my general inability to remain comfortable in strange places, and my inability to become alive anywhere else.

But then it is later and I am thinking again, picking through my brain and casting off the sloppy skins of its cover, terrorizing myself for not having accomplished enough, if anything, in my time here, and now with but a little more than a day left to wander about the city and attempt to discover something. But despite the teeth-gritting chastisement, I'm glad the trip is nearly over—valid or no. Certainly others, judging objectively (or, at least, from their detached subjectivity), would see little in the trip that was valid. I've learned nothing new about Esperanza, after all, or about anyone else I'm trying to thread into my story. They might rightly wonder if I am only acting. Only pretending to be a writer. An artist. Man. Human. Indeed, at this juncture I cannot deny that these roles are far beyond my diminishing skill as a thespian. Or is it, rather, that the audience has finally wised up? Perhaps it is a little (or a lot) of both. Two equally angled slopes passing by one another on converse lines of action—me in descent to meet the florid crowd ascending. I can catch the eye of one of these ascendant foes, brushing past on sidewalk, and receive the message instantly—fall off, already, you floundering fraud! Get lost! The waitress at Carlo's has been leery of me from the start, managing a smile as she brings me the menu that she knows I'll flip over again and again before ordering nothing but a café americano cargado, as I have done most days during my stay here. With her large, expectant eyes she reminds me a bit of a bartender who used to work at O'Reilly's Pub in the Heights east of Cleveland. Though the two, it seems, expected quite different things in reflection. Or maybe they didn't.

TROTSKY MURIÓ ANOCHE

The headline was a supreme shock, as if my entire body had been stroked with an electrified brush. It was a shock even though I headed to the newsstand that hot August morning fully expecting—hoping even, in certain corners of my mind—to find just such a pronouncement screaming at me from above the fold. Truth be told, I plunked down my 50 centavos or whatever with the same masochistic anticipation that had once driven me into a screening of a Revolutionary Eisenstein cut-up, to confirm that I had indeed gone missing from it. I'd have been disappointed to read that I was still lingering in some horrible, semiconscious state between life and death, or, even, that I had pulled through the worst and was now expected to make a full recovery. What would I—that is, the me here and now, the fugitive's fugitive—do then? Since my escape in May from the heat of the Siqueros attack I'd been living a life of subsistence, tucked away in the Parque Hundido, sleeping on benches, begging and digging in trashcans for food. After a couple of weeks, the fear of being recognized as the great Trotsky had all but vanished (after all, there was still a living, breathing cover carrying that mantle in the house in Coyoacán) and I woke one day from an afternoon nap and rolled over in the grass to an exhilarating, almost overwhelming sense of liberation. All at once it hit me that I was now perfectly free to walk or lounge about as I pleased, simply admiring the trees or the calls of the birds, or smile lying back in the grass with the heat of the sun lapping my face. The rolling history of humanity was no longer my concern. I was hardly even a member of humanity any longer. The revolution was over. I never dreamed one could slip away from it so easily, so unnoticed, with not a hint of consequences. The world spun on, grass grew, the clouds gathered and shed rain at a time humans call six o'clock, but, as I should have seen earlier, might just as well have been four or ten or any other number. It hardly mattered. And, to my utter surprise, not mattering, as it turned out, was one of the greatest experiences the world could possibly offer up.

But experiences are hard things to hold onto. (And this might go doubly for those who have physically divorced themselves from themselves.) This new, airy whiff of freedom that I had inhaled on the grassy slopes of Parque Hundido barely lasted out the week. After that I was sick again with worry. I no longer suffered from fears of being discovered (people, as I had learned over the preceding months, will see whomever they want in a face, and, even when they first see correctly, can, with little effort, be talked out of trusting the report given by their eyes), but now I was seized with the anxiety that I might, against my own will (if such a thing can even rightly be said to be at our command), slip (slowly or suddenly) back into my former self, without even distilling the forces that had allowed me to make the split in the first place. I might be swallowed up by the Old Man of the Fourth International and be ingested so completely—become blood of his blood—that I would forget that I had once run the filter of his skin and shot free. Worse, I would lose the rebellious desire that had made that propulsion away from him possible. Thus the anxiety grated on the sharp metal edges of that airy alternate reality and my ephemeral ability to remain within it, to successfully stay apart from my former self, to strike out and make a way for myself from scratch in a land that was still very much unfamiliar to me and, despite the bouts of fleeting lightheadedness, startlingly real and concrete. Could I manage to duck away quietly into this other life while that shell of a Trotsky—who, should he remain alive, would continue to be recognized as the genuine article—still puttered about the garden on calle Vienna and sent out revolutionary treatises culled from the Dictaphone cylinders littering his Coyoacán fortress?

La Policía Hará una Investigación

Minuciosa del Proditorio Asesinato

Of course they would. They'd make a big show of it. Pump themselves up for all their great detective work and lay it out for the world step by step, breath by breath, betrayal by betrayal. But what would it matter? Who could deny that the puppet strings ultimately led back to Stalin?

Tras la penosa y larga agonía, el exiliado ruso

falleció a las 19:25 horas

Painful. Long. Agony. The words carried no punch whatsoever. They were close to meaningless, in fact. I had died at 7:25 the previous evening, as the first proper sentence of the article explained: "León Trotsky murió a las 19 horas 25 minutos de ayer." The 25 hours I had lasted in the hospital had been full of painful agony. And now I was dead. Nonexistent. A factual nothing, even if I couldn't feel that nothingness or relate to it in any way. There I stood, motionless in front of the newsstand, reading and rereading the headline, the subheads, the opening sentences, trying without success to feel the agony, the blurry-headed, throbbing descent or expansion or implosion or whatever it was that I, he, Trotsky, had endured throughout the daylong ordeal. But I failed at every attempt. It was done, and I was separate. Ridiculously, impossibly separate. Here while he was there. Alive while he was dead. Alive while *I* was dead. It made no sense, but I couldn't even be bothered by the absurdity of not being bothered by the situation. I did, nonetheless, retain a strong enough sense of decorum to ask myself for at least some outward show of sorrow over my passing. But the tears refused to come. I was all dried out.

So instead of dripping I went lightheaded again and my form wavered in the morning air. Thick, sooty smoke lifted from the hair follicles in my scalp, and wax ran down from my forehead in quick, liquid threads that coagulated at the base of my neck and stepped back up to my jaw in cold, knobby protrusions. My ears hummed in terrifying hymnal glory. Gloria in excelsis gloria. Immense heat lit the core of my brain, burning away mass and memory from the inside out. Then I blanked completely. And after some unaccountable time—hours, weeks, months, years—emerged slowly as if pushing my head out through a thick batting of wool, finding my body reclined on a cot in a dark, basement dwelling, the light from a single bare-bulb lamp pushing its wattage out into the blackness from the center of a round table stationed on the other side of the room.

"You Showed Me the Way," recorded by Billie Holiday with Teddy Wilson and his Orchestra for the Brunswick label on Thursday, February 18, 1937 at the 1776 Broadway studio in New York City. Musicians: Billie Holiday, vocals; Henry "Red" Allen, trumpet; Cecil Scott, clarinet; Prince Robinson, tenor saxophone; Teddy Wilson, piano; Jimmy McLin, guitar; John Kirby, bass; Cozy Cole, drums.

Tinkling of piano at open. Clarinet solo breezes in warmly over piano swirls and chopping rhythm section. Deep, smooth and mellow, the clarinet, recalling late-evening nestling by young lovers on porch swings in summer. Then a brief piano solo, hopping around lightly, twirling. Trumpet cuts in with heated blare, swoops and repeats. And Billie sings (with clarinet cooing always underneath) *You showed me the way* ... her voice falling gently over the lilting rhythm like an afternoon rain, sprinkling the relaxed swing time with a dreamlike quality, opening time, as it were, to fall back on distant shadows and negate itself, while it expands still, drifting in all directions, a cozy flavor to fill the brain ... Then the trumpet back, brightly stamping the closing melody over the heartily swinging but grounded full band, and Fromm sits bolt upright— finally gets it. Shazam! *That* was the clarinet melody that had run through his head the day of the conference. Coming to him just before or after or when he (no doubt, mistakenly) saw Billie Holiday lingering at the back wall. That song. That breezy bittersweet song. The one that was playing on the radio the day his second wife, Henny, died. He was driving home from the hospital when it came on. Or was already home, sitting alone in the kitchen, hearing a radio he couldn't remember turning on. Or maybe he was …

The young waitress at Pan Comido, a small vegetarian joint on calle Tonalá, is a comfort for beat eyes in her UGGs, piercings and warm, flirtatious manner.

—Quieres cerveza? she asks, handing me the menu card as I take up a stool at the eating shelf that runs the length of one short wall in the place.

—No.

—Agua del día?

—Ah, no sé.

—Algo? she grins.

—Sí, algo, I laugh. Un café, creo.

—Ah no, no tenemos café ahora.

—Hmm. OK. I scan the menu briefly for no good reason. Entonces, qué es el agua del día?

—Es piña, con alguna otra fruta. No recuerdo exactamente. Pero está buenísima.

—OK, muy bien. Sí, tengo eso.

—Bueno.

The menu is an assortment of sandwiches and salads named after Western celebrities and historical figures: ensalada Madonna, ensalada Newton, sandwich Morrissey, falafel Lennon or Yoko Ono, hamburguesa Da Vinci. When the cute, earthy waitress returns with my flavored water (making a point of informing me that, besides the pineapple, there's also mango in the drink) I order the Morrissey, a sandwich of asparagus and three different cheeses, topped with a three-chile pesto. She approves and goes to place the order. At the counter, she jokes now with the other waitress. Laughing about me, no doubt. For, indeed, I am something of a gringo clown today in my Mexican football jersey and stammering, bungled Spanish. And by jotting notes now and then in my palm-sized notebook, perhaps they think I'm an American travel writer, trying comically to blend in, and the waitress's friendliness is but an angle to get good mention in my book. Well, here it is, churrita, though I doubt this is the book you had in mind.

But, no, she was friendly from the start. And now she comes over and tells me she can, in fact, make me a coffee, if I'd still like one. The caffeine demon snaking around my forehead readily accepts, and the waitress returns in a few minutes with a freshly prepared coffee in a single-serving French press—a welcome departure after days of americanos that, to mis labios estadounidenses, are always too small. I finish the savory asparagus sandwich with the pineapple-mango water, then sit for a while reading the June issue of the Universidad de México magazine—its articles all devoted to the recently deceased Carlos Fuentes—as I finish my coffee.

But the place (at least there at the shelf) is not especially conducive to lingering. So I finish quickly, pay my bill (wondering if the tip will appear excessive—whether it *is*, in fact, excessive—but, then, what of it?), pop the mint from the bill tray into my mouth, respond to my waitress's wave and gracias with those of my own and head out.

Before returning to my hotel, I duck into la Librería Gensania, the bookstore there next to Pan Comido, and browse the tightly lined shelves back into the bowels of the shop, to the low-ceilinged, basement-like portion of the place, and somewhere in those crowded stacks locate a copy of César Aira's *Los dos payasos*, which I buy for 34 pesos and leave happy to take up again my gringo parade of streets in the slant of midafternoon shadows, following someone who no longer exists.

Hearing her knuckles rap against the metal door reminded Esperanza of the dead hollow thunk produced from knocking on the old iron door at the house on calle Redondas. But that was after Dave died, and the horror began. Really began. The horror that eventually led her here. Or had *meeting* Dave been the trigger that kicked her down this path? She knocked. There was movement inside. Or there wasn't. A shot of air, with stench (like?) descended the stairs (how many?) and immediately rustled through her hair, bristling the nape of her neck. Six? The smell that rose each morning from the dirt floor of casita Redondas: earth and coldness and the regenerating molecules of lost life. Eight. She knocked. And there was a creak. From the door or inside? In her mind? She shivered. But if he didn't want her story or wouldn't go for it, in whole or in part, there was nothing she could do about it. He might need convincing, he might accept it outright or reject it just as quickly. There was no telling. Though something convinced her that he not only would be eager to hear what she had to say, but would find her plan most agreeable to boot. Anxious himself, too? Certainly. It was possible. When did she knock last? Was he coming? Was he here even? A trap? Did Borges know already? No, impossible. He must be at least an hour behind her. Una hora y media tal vez. Once she and Ramón failed to show up at the rendezvous point, Borges would get the call and then he'd be on her like shit. She knocked. Well, he'd be on Ramón first off, finding his forehead split open and leaking into the basement carpet. The crowbar jutting up from the lump of cranial mass on the floor. Jutting up at a 45-degree angle like a sprig once sprouted from a root ball that was now decaying into the mossy forest floor. That sprig itself quickly dying, stiffening hard and naked. Or had she dislodged it? Yes, there she was, setting the crowbar quietly beside the slain body. She remembered noting that the bar stretched nearly the length from the top of the man's skull to his waist. Though not quite. She felt again the stiffness in her lower back from bending over to place the crowbar on the carpet and the twinge from rising again. Or was she feeling it now for the first time? And the tool, then, after all (despite the memory she had been quite certain of just a moment earlier), remained stuck where she had planted it in the stalker Ramón's skull. Or had the pain in her lower back, perhaps, been recalled from an entirely different, though closely connected, event—namely that earlier series of actions that found her lowering the bag of complex onto the basement sofa, then stooping to draw the crowbar out from beneath the sofa (where she had placed it a few days earlier) and rising again and walking the handful of required paces to position herself in the most appropriate spot—the spot most advantageous, most athletically apt—to await Ramón's descent down stairs and his turning into the square-on, have-at-me stance, whereupon she stepped forward to deal with deadly intent (a more easily, more smoothly and strongly rehearsed remembrance by limb and spine to bend with full graceful force into the slaying blow never could she recall in all her days of performing repeated—let alone, athletic—actions) the swing downward necessary for the hoeing of cortical dirt. Again she took up the complex. And hoisting the shoulder bag upon her person, looked down upon the stricken one there splayed on carpet and dripping, and said unto him, Don't you remember this. And with that passing comment, she left and went out. She knocked. Tunk tunk tunk. Ta-tunk. And again the silence of space and waiting and the advancing pressure hatched from the womb of the hollow metal door, ballooning from the oxidized inner to cast its throbbing shadow o'er her like those bulbous thumbs that had once expanded her childhood dreams (recalled to her later upon seeing that inflated gray hand in Tamayo's *Mujeres cantando*), weighing down her hands and finally, through their sheer volume, forcing the rest of her body from the dream frame or pressing it into a tight corner, where it was crushed by the heavy, buzzing weight of silence. And then the latch, working now in a bolt of sonorous action and the feeling even of something slipping loose in her stomach and being tugged. Then the extra-black sliver between the door and frame. And his face working out from the rough stitching of darkness.

—Piochitas, she cooed.

—Get your ass through the door, he muttered gruffly.

Inside, space was cool and stale, and bluely dark. She followed the old man's curved figure, drawn by its gray, pixelated splotches, shuffling ahead through the darkness toward a yellow light in the distance—the glow now radiating a thick hallow about the man's wiggling form as if the two together—hallow and body—formed a distressed, jaundiced vulva. Till both he and the light took on a more definitive character: the man sketched now in his mid-sixties, ramrod straight and fit, the bristly point of his white goatee licking from the chin of what seemed a glowing gold mask; the flat light loosed from a lantern that, in the yellow clarity wiping away the room's muddy darkness, appeared to be made of paper. The burden of identifying the figures that flickered in and out of solid form caused her head to thump like a drum. The paper lantern burned cold and bright like the moon. Without waiting for his instruction or request she approached the table—for table it proved roundly to be, supporting the lantern at its center—and set her shoulder bag down upon it. She folded back the bag's opening and looked at him. The bag, multiplied by two in the round lenses of his glasses, expanded as he leaned in over the table. His eyes blinked heavily beneath the canvas bundles. He hummed in various tonal configurations as he inspected the bag's contents, his fingers playing lightly over the satchel's folded opening. Then he closed the bag abruptly and looked up at her, his visage contorted either by shock or by the sharp re-angling of light as it struck his features.

—Based on our earlier correspondence, I'd anticipated something different, he said, the clay of his jaws operating with a commanding, milky strength. I had no idea you were going to take it in this direction.

—It's only natural, she grinned. This seemed to disturb him further, and he shook his head vigorously.

—It's not what I expected.

Then he took up the bag and stepped back from the table, sinking for a moment into shadow (did she hear a labored exhalation from the darkness?) before resurfacing.

—And it'll work out okay if we follow this? he asked.

—It'll work, she smiled. You needn't worry about that. You can cross any border following that script.

He nodded repeatedly, but his manner betrayed a lack of confidence.

—What specifically is your complaint?

—It just seems too incredible.

—You're showing your age, she laughed. Maybe you're stuck in the past after all.

He forced a grin, but it was laced more with disgust and cruelty than with accepting humor. Or maybe the harsh, funhouse shadows were yet again misshaping his emotions.

—I suppose I'm at your service, he relented. I have little choice but to trust your calculations at this point.

—Oh, don't sound so defeated, she chided, feeling quite cruel herself now. Things change. I'd have thought that little piece of wisdom would've found its way into your skull by now. We all had our ideas about certain things in the past, but most of them proved to be nonsense. She motioned toward the bag. This is how things are moving now. This is how we get into the United States, I assure you. But if you want to talk about it some, we can do that. The last thing I want is for you to feel I'm pushing you to take all this on some kind of faith.

—No, no, I trust you, he said, then added with forced emphasis: And trust is quite a different matter than faith.

—Indeed it is, she groaned. I'm glad we can agree on that.

He nodded, sending the shadows on his face into slow, stretching motion.

—So when do we go?

—I had thought it better be tonight.

Trotsky's carnival mask now leaked serious mistrust from the depths of its swirling shadows.

—Why the urgency?

Esperanza Villanueva smiled a bit and immediately knew it was the wrong response.

—It didn't go as you said with Ramón, did it?

—Things with Ramón rarely go as you plan.

—It's not a joke, he scolded. If you had to do it, you had to do it. But it's not a matter for jokes.

—As you wish.

He grinned sadly, his lips carving deeply into his cheeks.

—Ah, but you're beyond listening, aren't you? This old man is already baggage to the likes of you.

—Not beyond listening, Piochitas. I'm beyond worshiping, yes.

—Chingada madre, he exhorted, turning away into the darkness. I never asked for that.

There was a harsh swiveling of the light, and then he was bobbing away with the lantern. Esperanza followed him. It was a long way going, spiraling down stairs, floating through doors, sliding down mossy stone tunnels that looped the pair smoothly up to the ceiling, over and down again as if riding screw-like threads. Their jaunt pushed its way well beyond the limits of the building's physical dimensions. But hours or minutes later Trotsky finally stopped. He extended his left arm out behind him to stall her motion as well. They stood facing a rusting, iron door, to which Trotsky now applied his right ear. He hummed a low drone as he listened, a meditative mantra of sorts that seemed to Esperanza wholly out of character for the old war commissar. But after a time, he stepped back and, without warning or explanation or further hesitation, flung the door open to a barreling rush of loud sunlight. He turned back to Esperanza, his eyes blinking rapidly.

—The only thing I might add before we go on, he called as if projecting his voice into a gusting wind, is to remind you that I've been in these shoes before. I awoke once too, you know. This isn't my first time fleeing. In fact,

I've been fleeing most of my life. So I know a thing or two about it. And if I'm certain of anything now, it's that crossing this border is bound to mix things up.

—Yes, I'm sure you're right, she responded impatiently. But, whatever happens, the official story is that I've never been here. You never saw me. Are we straight on that? When we go our separate ways on the other side it will be like ...

III

TRISTEZA ESPERANZA

Tristessa, O Yé, comme t'est Belle

—Jack Kerouac, *Tristessa*

OUT FROM SWADDLING MAYBE BUT WHO CAN REMEMBER WHEN FIRST YOU PEEK and what you see feel know or care about if a thing but warmth and filling your belly which it takes years struggling away from to realize that's all there ever is if only in other guises cloaked by adverbial half notes in croon or by muck by blood or some other sticky bodily excretion and sweat in needles plumbing worn flesh it all comes round every bit of it so that hope is but hope for returning to the womb which is death.

Once I walked and the sky was clear blue a wind whistled in the leaves over my head and my clothes were pressed I skipped I think long concrete paths over littering of crumpled papers and black oil stains stepped to Azteca oom-pa and bells in my head twirling a brightly colored umbrella humming aloud going to you to your café and your coffee.

It seizes you hard the first time it takes waves of heat crashing under your skin over and over breaking on the grains of your childhood to cast in the rush and begin the erosion then the amazing emptiness afterwards where everything is serenely clear but void waiting for you to answer it the vast cosmic question in an instant that you curse that oil that brought you here left you on this beach to pray to misunderstanding and want the breeze always blowing outward at your back.

He took my hand across the table and began it like later the prick now the thumb massaging the young muscles of my forearm kneading them to rest that they might want to live forever feeling this way and smiled eyes over me burning some ancient understanding that elevated people up pyramids and grazed fields of flowers and fruit and canalled waterways to flood the lowlands when needed or cleared timber with fire all in the magic of knowing Mother Earth and her longings and flow caressing her to a climax in the weak moment she lay down to our evolution.

I had a sucker When? but then three or four years of age and I stood holding the brightly colored circle on stick like the girl in the park by Rivera in her finery tho I never could've been like that still the memory paints with the varnish of our feeling so I did I did stand like that once licking and content and the world was open to me even as los indios were being tossed around me by the collar and la Catrina paraded nearby in her plumage.

And a bicycle which I learned to ride early and tore up and down the crumbling of our streets bumping in light dress and shoeless squealing delight bringing people outofdoors to shake heads or begin laughing pointing as the old bike hopped precariously over large stones in the pavement and tossed me like rag doll to and fro down a hill and faster.

Till papá took me aside one sticky polluted morning and chided me briskly and slapped me about a bit introducing me in his swearing to mis senos y mis muslos the girl dress stripped from me suddenly in the pronouncement of my sin not en realidad but in the clarity of my knowing the sin in bounce the sin in elevation and wind and fearlessness.

But it was Diego himself I think now and not some little girl not myself then couldn't be but I can't fight it can't rearrange the memory or reshape the dream of it so I stand in childhood in short pants (not in dress at all) like Rivera in the way he remembers or recasts his youth in oils.

So after that it was different (how couldn't it be?) so painfully selfaware dressing loosely at first to cover it then with a defiance born of rage over what I eventually took as a binding of my soul as it'd be done with feet to keep it small dressing loosely to expose myself as shapely as possible evoking surviving the rage of papá till he grew tired of it disparagingly giving me up for lost disowned.

All I ever loved in school was to read ignoring the other subjects in order to ingest otra novela hidden inside the pages of my other texts Math Science Espiritualidad all the time reading dreaming drifting from the wood and nails of my everyday existence to trace the path of clouds unraveling from limitless space inside my mind.

Then by hand he took me and led me from the café in his grip led down broad streets with sun still and passersby then into the slim callecitas framed by stone buildings reaching on either side up so they looked to be leaning over at the top and swaying in the afternoon air looking to clap together and shower their broken rocks down on top of us to laughter then into what appeared to be nothing more than cracks left by poor construction but finally to a steel door near the end of one of them and in to a moist couch and roosters meeting for the first tho certainly not the last time my man.

Dave held me afterwards the warm clasp of V of arms tucking me into the pit of nirvana and flipping me over through the pure clear water air while the tongues of agave plants licked at our thighs and elbows pressing us deeper into the echoing pleasure of the space left by the taking of the drug then released me and I tumbled alone going ever deeper unafraid the sculpture of my flesh disappearing allowing me to flow out into the immensity of all being losing myself yet retaining the sense of knowledge increasing always at coming into being perpetually till I went beyond this and everything went black and I woke later in Dave's old-man loose grip a scrawny evileyed cock on the floor between my legs screaming nightmares.

My mother took me aside one day by the arms and spread them out for herself to see for sure to know what she must've expected for months and there was the proof of it plain to see in her eyes the pain to know the life you've wrecked is not only your own.

I played once in the yard and there was a frog hopping between the blades of grass and I reached down to stroke his bumping shoulders he skipped into the brush of my finger and each time I reached down to him he did the same even waiting for me on those times I held back to see if it was but coincidence and would he hop on but he didn't only flapped his eyelids as if to clear his vision and make sure he had not somehow simply lost sight of my finger in some blur and when I once again did lower it he'd spring so it'd scare me the quickness of his knowing in not thinking in-tune more to the universe than I ever could be thru awareness.

Then I read via García Lorca of the great mirror doming above us Man is blue he wrote.

Amen I said. Hosanna he said.

She pushed up the sleeves of my sky blue dress with the ruffles at the wrists and inspected but no couldn't have the dress being that I'd received for my eighth birthday and wore incessantly till the elbows and collar wore out so maybe it was this my mother was inspecting and perhaps the dismayed scowl to lips was but the result of a needle gripped there ready to be set to my sleeves with thread the scorched memory again mixed up with one earlier and what I've toiled over in cavernous corners with things dripping somewhere everywhere around me vast sinking guilt over what I've made of myself and what it's caused was spawned always by an inaccurate remembrance of facts maybe things that never even happened only monsters of self-devouring affliction always hungry always growing twisting my brain in its claws to rearrange the coiled goop into an army against myself.

We were sitting in an open green space under a grouping of two or three trees a place I remember as the love park in la Ciudad Universitaria which it couldn't have been it not existing yet and he pressed his thumb into my palm and asked me if I'd ever that which so childishly I'd never even thought of but for something distant adults played out in hidden rooms the allatonce acknowledgement that here it was on me suddenly his hand running up my thigh.

I began writing letters for no known reason never sent them but tucked all of them away in the same envelope one after the other till that envelope filled over and I had to start me another and filed it away in the top drawer of my dresser never again to read anything I'd written.

Nights were with Dave then always awake drifting into some chemically induced dream that drifted itself into something resembling sleep just before dawn and ended a few hours later in the sudden jolting awake to a pallid hollow inside everything ridiculously clear the outlines distinct the innate separateness of all the makeup of the world discovered in an instant as before I'd discovered it but let melt away in the flooding of foreign substances into my bloodstream here it was again alive screaming at me poking me with its edges forcing me to know in my empty pain I was always and would always en realidad be alone.

So what was it she said to me on that occasion or did she say a thing or just go about her motherly duties as I not knowing then would never in my life be able to do barely in the soft dream of mi muñeca able always leaving her be in the most precarious of places till she caught once finally in the sparks of the oven and extinguished herself in a rage of fire and was gone probably be one of those that unknowingly in a fit of mental collapse took her offspring to the river or tub to hold them under and remove all connection to the continuing cycle of life and its everrenewing toil.

He read books this other man I met once somehow clear in my head then and unnervous enough to sit with him over several hours and discuss the purpose of writing of which I knew nothing but in the sway of his grip seemed knowledgeable knowing even and spoke intelligently of things which I had really only the slightest idea about so perhaps I wasn't so clear then as I thought or think now I was maybe none of it made any sense but was right with him and for a moment as those hours lasted there indeed seemed to be some purpose some noble approach to life that didn't sacrifice the useless pain of it all but met up with it somehow and stuck sword to it and pierced back delaying or maybe hastening the killing of it all which in the end is the same.

Papá was away a lot to places I don't know where leaving mother and me alone together for days or weeks at a time absorbing each other's company in the silence of polluted afternoons at our chores or she there with me playing with the doll when I still had it or what guilty quite often at the neverendingness of her toil while I sat on the floor on the rug always under her legs seemingly she silent stepping aside and continuing or continuing to work right there above me which grew in time worse than any scolding the press of her Catholic sacrifice to man and God and shouldn't I be doing something to help tearing at the alternate feeling in my stomach that I should defiantly remain where I was do nothing but as a child play chase away any feeling of remorse de inútil de recriminación directed squarely on self and live simply live!

The landlady's daughter was the opposite of myself with hair trimmed neatly at the shoulders and short white socks played with me tho I don't remember how it was we met who introduced but in streets under the watch of metal cans and discarded iron garters propped against walls of crumbling brick rivets still in but sawed from at the edge from what once they were connected she in a steady stream of conversation of inanities about her doll and the one she had given to me and I always in follow-up trying to match her bubbling in glassedover sparkling eyes to all life and social order decaying around her but played and believed it and moved on I think because of it her willful ignorance tho maybe never even had to make such a choice spin to her brain and attitude but simply born like that and prospered because of it got out later and never needed to look back at the rest of us drowning in the sludge.

Then one night papá came home mother nowhere to be found which seems odd now as I always have the nagging feeling of her always at elbow tugging annoyingly at it but she was suddenly gone this time and papá came home in the half-light and was there something foul on his breath or was there not was he sweaty or freshly showered he wore a tie I think but not a jacket with the tie loosened around an open collar he took me.

But what did you expect? Did you not see it coming? As I did not see and he did not see till we looked back on it later?

He left for a long time after that and mother sat worrying her stomach away I dare not tell what had passed between me and papá for the damage I knew it would do her she trapped ever stitching away the minutes of her life and would be till the end that it dawned on me suddenly then how much more afflicted she was by papá than I tho maybe she never felt the piercing jolt every time he brushed by the slightest touch of our clothes' fabric once he finally did return home to suffer together our separate silent pact or maybe she did maybe every day of her life it was there shocking her wearing her down till by now she could no longer feel it only the emptiness from the pain days he wasn't around.

That look last seen on her by me least ways at her looking down on him and he up tho not looking but up dead nothing the whitish hue to the skin stretched now on his face then falling plastic into the crevices at his cheeks and powdered the kinetic energy still pulsing beneath the surface to gather soon and explode I thought as a grouping into motion and become itself unthinkable to feel him not knowing not feeling to've been wiped clean dry and empty no longer responsible then for what he had done for nothing that even in the slightest motion of a finger now forever laid dormant had been perpetrated or brushed over with kindness none of it the snap thought and blood feeling behind any action a history closed to dusty book pages but bone or if as could be the other thinking the rage did still soar and left with him to continue elsewhere to be forgiven or not my hatred would go with it not to be cleansed but to fester *fester* in incensed catacombs of heart and rot it in an outward path going claiming every vein eventually with its decaying blackness such were the choices not flickered on Mother's face but under the surface of mine she empty no doubt for the duration by the dying of her jailor I the cranker of key to the cogs for the turning of stomach mine own.

Did I write more after that? No. Did I miss it? No. But read some still. Would I live so he Jack would make me immortal in the writing of his? Yes, so it'd happen. But no.

I went to Dave then and he was glad in my coming little I'd noticed it before but till that night and looked back discovering the worldopening pleasure in the look on his face for the look on my face that I learned to make it automatic intentional instead of by chance and had him for good spell of a time till I forgot and got weak let syrup jelly my arms and my legs and my chest till my heart pumped it as sludge to my brain and I forgot and let him back on top of me and for the last ever to his submission anything he'd say my mangod my corrupter my savior my all for the glory of junk up the arm or the ass wherever I could stick it and bow to him and murmur and know in a teary sweat from my pores how holy it was and he was and the destruction of life was and dying was and yes that it does indeed go on forever and forever.

A candle lit in my heart and I felt it flicker behind the red bubbled casing unsteady breeze caused it to dance torpid then flutter.

You are the wick shoved thick and longing.

It was a normal day overly dry and sunny and walking on sidewalk somehow missing my bus so that the back of my tongue grew arid and spread into the back of my throat causing me to swallow hard several times while walking then sweat profusely since I was off the junk also somehow but not completely bad for it walking in the sun showing possible walkways to the future and what could really so easily be if I turned and trotted up to the university there or completed preparatoria even registered for classes and sat in on the learning of things and plotted a career path over years and years into my future now moving off into darkness and what could it be but for long hours in the studying and what was there really ever to learn that I didn't already know walking with the feel of the hot concrete radiating up thru my shoes and all those hot steps to get there even if I did learn and it was worthwhile all the hot steps till my feet were scarred from em and having knowledge no longer wanted to walk what then what then no I don't think so not for me jamás never it couldn't ever be meant for me.

And it was around that same time that I went into the church and knelt back among the candles and gazed thru the heavy bronzed air at nothing at wood at stationary figures somehow passing away into the corners as the shadows of flickering candles and prayed perhaps tho I can't for the life of me remember what for or how or if or why and then I was outside again and the sky was very clear and the sun shone down as when I'd entered and the people and cars and buses moved as always.

And later that day but why I remember this I have no way of knowing but do remember and am sure that it was tho insignificant later that afternoon that I slipped with a chopping knife and sliced my finger the quick blood pooling smoothly on the halved lime I'd cut citric acid soon swallowing its red thickness.

We were married later weeks months tho it lasted only a short while till he died but forever after lighting candles to reevoke him my protector my angel so that the time we had together in reality is mixed with the after and flips back and forth expanding love into this eternity filled with pain and sickness and relief through a needle flickering in your vein I will always and do love you Dave.

I don't remember the next man touching me only finishing and smoking a long time before reaching for his wallet black leather unfolded finally in fat palm owing to my first incurable silence and what must've seemed dead stare into space so I spooked him probably as I spooked myself and continued to do it to light again that burning in my middle as a torture to lick my insides with sting of guilt singe the tubes that carry blood and puss and shit all that makes us human earthly dirt longing for the Virgin's tears to cleanse me which I did not deserve and so I kept at it to feel the guilt and the rest always knowing what I'd become knowing the punishment I had coming to me dealt by my very own hand as a saint dying long and hard and always His and his my Dave so that one day maybe I might meet him again in the sweet injection of heaven.

Next day I went to see Jack since I was broke and sick and why? I ended up offering myself to him why? since both of us were nothing and but lost separately in separate nothingnesses he to his Buddha and me to what? was? longing only for junk but maybe in a moment both of us for the rubbing of souls on the mattress nada to nada into nada and the glory of it restrained only by our separate pure leanings toward destruction toward the scraping of our hollows as by rakes sharply tonged forks to make us raw worthy bleeding nothing a life of pain as life should be and is.

And he was gone for a year then only writing softest letters that I couldn't believe any of his expression could be of this earth truly but existed only truly in his letters which I returned the best I could in kind the last letters the last writing in fact I'd ever write which did tho have the effect so he said of making him return after that year had passed and everything and all time had passed and I was somehow into it then with Bill chasing junk as always he on the same dreaded so glorious trail as myself dying together and so unavoidably together in other ways too tho rarely only whenever each of us had the required energy built up the physical need simply for release that gushing out in the order of things much as gushing in the constant physical cycle of the drain and its pump babump ah pish.

We stayed all that night once with Cruz succumbing mi hermana to sidewalk sleep and Jack shivering the justbeforedawn shiver over and over I laughing at him and feeding him more of the warm punch when all he wanted was a bed to drift into anywhere his brakeman arms wrapped about my junksick wasted girl form when all I wanted needed was junk waking Cruz then to stumble off into the morning tween those off to the office slitherin tween them and into darker crevices every place we walked into Jack searching for a bed so it became a game to me but really for morphine shot sweet in the arm finally finding it in den with bed so big Jack's eyes were bursting but I rolled up my coat sleeve and ...

That's when I died on him later so he says and wrote but to me it was just a dropping and if he'd seen the times before when he was away shoulda let me go just let and he soon enough after anyway so he shoulda but in great ego Buddha twist didn't took me in arms wrapped me prayed like once I'd prayed but no more prayed in selfish oneway love to keep me there with him and did so he says and wrote and I stayed or came back and was there again and got up and walked he and Cruz and I like risen saints into yellow Mexican morning so he wrote or shouldhave.

But I told him later that Bill was for me not him not Jack Bill the nonlover junky junk man with the money keep me sweep me bee me.

So he injected me shall I say sedated like the rest but I let him have it.

Free.

And the next time I ratataptapped on that Orizaba flat there wasn't Jack and I knew no more would ever be relaxed ingested secanols and went mad black furniture thru air and windows Bill tumbling screaming gone waking then in calm sidewalk birds singing people in fine pressed clothing stepping over me for work and lives I paralyzed for long time after fore I could stand it recalibrate my bearings for stumblewalk home thru treelined hours.

To more pain more dens more black more junk more needles and swallows nothingness in the making of money by the parting or forcing or allowing of legs hanging limp counting it out while they were still sweating each flip of each bill snapping stiffness in my veins rousing me off to buy the sludge to soften and cool those inner pathways talktalktalking.

But it ends as it must ends.

Nothing.

Which is nothing.

Into nothing.

Dead.

Tho you don't realize it then only nothing to look back on later wonder about feel thickly till it expands in your temples and forehead threatens to inflate back and retake you sit down rest and let it pass breathe breathe.

So I can't say how long I was really out or the situation in particular that put me in that state when where how who with what done to me then unknowing uncaring for sure dying dead and lying nor what rose me what dream evoked me whose call from where why when and cleansed me.

I was alive when I woke peeled the sheet back lightly and dry like the soft skin of a tomatillo from my green body fresh sprung from the cool bed to stretch and restart my day which was my life renewed and beckoning me how many tens of years later to relive it.

So I walked out the door of that strangely abandoned flat there at Orizaba 210 stepped onto the bright sidewalk y doblé a la derecha up cross streets past the fountain in the Plaza Luis Cabrera sparkling the morning sunlight the noise wonderful cool but then blending with noise incredible I just noticed placed cars whizzing by in a fashion I'd never that I stopped without realizing it and the fountain roared into all sights of kids running by in clothes manufactured by in between paths of sleekly hewn plastic cars and metal screeches of sound thru opened windows pounding noise and beat what smoothly swiping corner and was gone I stood dumb the only thing in the whole world apparently now silent drinking in the lappings of the fountain's spray at its pool quiet for how long no knowing guessing what this world was with as I soon discovered later high glass buildings rising to the clouds and smog and all manner of commerce in square sculpted buildings and metal glass noise speed lights rushing off between trees into the whole of oncoming future.

At a certain point I began again walking noticing now for the first time in my life the clap of my own footstep to the concrete tapping this slight lifebeat neath hum and boom of giant life spreading out over realm of all existence here I was simply walking me and being noticed by myself if no one else and so more so by myself more alone and alive than ever walking clacking making my way north up along Orizaba crossing by carelessness and heartgasp first then by relaxing and look rushing the clearing to center of street then passing over second half the same past the Casa Lamm restaurant and bookstore which used to be what? when? smiling walking more quickly emerging onto the plaza of David Dave I thought lighting candles all bronzed and confident in his nakedness fished my pockets for pesos suddenly but found nothing realizing without fear yet tho how helpless and alone I was in this freak world a dream where you know it's a dream and keep walking unhungry or needing of money keep walking and this land this concrete and brick passes quickly and might start you flying so you'll be over the mountains fore you know it walking on clouds floating admiring the metal stone cardboard glass boxes stretching out to the ends of the earth everywhere below you.

I floated down remember coming up over hill of dirt tween paths of nopales stretched stiff and padded like mitts sprouting out from the earth bent at point and crouched took one in hand wrestled it free then carefully sucked on it avoiding needles picked them sank teeth into green meat of cactus and swallowed juice like dirty rain jam slick in its spillage.

The sun was what got me drove away good cheer of having woken now different me outside of time mine own and so like not counting no chance of mistake in life beyond the one that you're living free pass to do as you please and are better for it do less feel less like doing things that are evil less like destroying yourself and all the stopped up gunk in your veins feels open no matter mistake making a life other than your own with no ties to past or future but blowing that when you feel no need to make of yourself you have no need to take for yourself and tear others down but that cactus that grew there for you and all stretching to the horizon flat neath hollow mocking blue empty clear sea with the sun bobbing in it to burn you welcomes you in first with good cheer and warmth till you're too deep looking around suddenly to the whole in all directions unconcerned oven has you trapped laughing.

Pressed on tho for what could I do what can one do but continue into pits of passing shade just enough to brush the remembrance of some forgotten life love down thru your hair like fingers stroking so you might step once more one more step up again plant foot into giving dirt submit yourself to its sinking and try to rise to plant other and so on and over up sweating in sun pushing on you but somewhere back in some time someone other live suffering being touched and brushed you like that and fell so you lift up and go on toiling stepping wearing yourself ragged to find such a pocket of time once again and ride it like a bull heaving off into the wilting sunlight.

She'd go up then somehow continue cross those sun drenched lands and mountains stop off in little villages as sun sank down perhaps catching ride from workers returning bunched in rattling pickup whistling or just walk in and up to some door be shown kindness like never taken in given all the food she wanted and sleep on mattress of some fashion even when it seemed the family there was bursting every plank of the poor abode still they'd make room send her off in the morning with tortillas and meat to munch on the way even as they seemed to have nothing even amid protests she should stay amid laughter or tears people living a very poor very simple very tiring life caring only for people but something'd always drag as if her belly'd grown a hook with a cable on it reeling her in from the North she went out on dry roads over mountains somehow on mule perhaps or stuck to the road maybe and as said before owing to her much strengthened form and beauty skin from all years of restorative sleep dreaming away every grain of junk often got rides from the men driving by with large smiles and banda music blaring from cheap speakers heading north always north thru Querétaro and San Luis Potosí north up into the silver hills of Zacatecas then up 49 into Jiménez and Chihuahua and north finally into Juárez then across the border and into El Paso.

How would she cross there's no telling having never crossed myself on foot but once many years ago as a child still in grade school and that as an American heading south for the day with the family with money bought a Coca-Cola shopped and came back in summer shorts and printed T-shirt in and out of Nogales maybe or Agua Prieta or Sonoyta or somewhere smaller not on map along the border with Arizona the small church along the way in the desert with the sculpted figures of medieval dying Christ sculpted Mary eyes turned up to heaven in agonistic ecstasy the wood of Catholic sorrow that Mexico scared and always pulled me back misery of life twisting in me so how'd I know how she crossed poor Mexican waif in clothes undoubtedly tattered and since when had bath of some sort but maybe was able to wash just before passing over straighten up her act but still no papers no identification that wouldn't be 40 years outdated if she ever had such but in Juárez certainly could score some fake I.D. or smugglers to take her cross but for money and so how but perhaps if only I've seen too many movies perhaps became submerged somehow in the drug trade thinking she could wax her way free of it once she had what she needed or tried to play them or what but seems as logical a place as any for it to go wrong again and prove that the therapists are right and once a junky always a junky or a drunk that even after 40 years of restful sleep a half-life to blink away the awful baggage of life and this life in particular still you could slide back just like that forget the pleasure of walking free of it in the sun mind suddenly scrambled again meat flesh longing for prick for sustenance substance being all you are or ever will be in what's flowing now thru your just hardened veins via too fast pumping heart you're back and what won't anything you do just to have more of it stroke yourself on to heights of what if not but dying and longing for it?

So this is where I'll put her down again across the border already running frantic junked out again searching searching for that only one thing that'll make her whole we see.

She would've worked her way up the border then of Pacific crashing on beaches sometimes sleeping on thru the day but eventually trudging on after somehow hitching undoubtedly making it out of Texas and Arizona and Colorado to land herself here in California as every story goes and goes again waking one morning with cold Pacific waves lapping at her filthy clothes rub her eyes to the morning sun get up and move on bumming coins and scraps of food befriending stray dogs and sometimes bedding down with them at night to find them gone in the morning and move on quick bathing in the ocean then warming in the sun stomach grumbling first time this morning go out looking for morphine or heroin or crack they had now or meth all the new mindspinning choices but her credit the same to cash again and again in some makeshift bed feeling nothing till the needle once more hit stretching stretched skin inflating her like a football wiping clear all trace of stomach pain jabbing better than food for it stopped time or pushed forward beyond the reaches of ticking spinning always clock straight out zooming to float easy then nowhere and worry no how no more.

He picked her up one morning on the beach literally that is not for the sexual but an arm under each of hers and lifted drug her off to the bed of his truck where he leaned her struck her lightly few times smiled when she came round waited while the fog lifted both literally and figuratively both inside and out that is over dawn on the beach and dawn murmurings neath her skin of a feeling once spoke about as love tho she fought it mightily at first struggled free from his grip slapped backhand back cross his cheek and glared foul eyes bout to jump from her skull and run ragged ore his face burrow in singe paths of quick burning death in his brain but he simply laughed at her striking her dumb wondering only at who had found her why for how long never having felt so much like in fact never she could recall a trapped animal small helpless in his grasp nor the conflict of perhaps in the easiness of it wanting it wanting him just to hold her till in the next screaming flight and battling wrists at his shoulders screaming maybe outside or in only with ice sweat wanting so badly only to kill forever outrun that sick feeling even crack poets sing about as the end all while it's only screaming now banal giving up to the cradle death not acknowledged OUT let me and she battled but he laughed at her and held her more tightly whispered for a silence calm he said the grip loosening on her then but she remained and sank a bit the worst of it passed just looked at him softening in the retreating mist and listened for this once she listened and heard his voice tug the fissure of her lungs.

He drove me then up the coast sun streaking smudged windshield coolest warm breeze blowing in opened window held my hand sometimes just let it slip from the wheel to cover mine resting dead beside him brought it to life somehow meaning took it away from me my hand the arm gone asleep as in a dream and living by extension with some other unseen body this magic existence so they call it project it on screens sing about always that light shehand was alive because of it because of him and I watched wondered at such a feeling if I'd just forgotten or had ever so we drove a long while in this fashion with the sun peeking in thru splotches light film brushing of mud wondering if ever this'd happened before and how where.

I have work for you he said can find it anyway if you're at all interested cleaning and such but can hook you up certainly no problem with papers as and he laughed and the cigarette on his lip bounced so he felt compelled to steady it tween two fingers and grin some more inhale coolly drew cigarette from lips exhaled quick swirl in a heavy white stream pulled out the window and replaced smoke to lip where it bounced more as he spoke in the rasp as it's chic somehow now for these rich bitches to hire the illegals bout as rebellious as they get I suppose cept for banging the hubby's law partner or golf partner or neighbor's wife or something but that's about it he laughs so yeah piece of cake I could line ya up right away not a thing to it you'll see if ya wanta.

At that point I suppose I just looked at him didn't give him yes or a no for an answer but smiled maybe and we drove on he accepting it all not bothered by my silence in fact easing into it quite naturally becoming silent himself just driving fiddling with the radio occasionally calm no notion no doubt of the chaos I'd bring into his life later the middle of night freakouts high on what what not slashing wrists in a terror really only to force on him the trouble of patching me up wanting to see how long he'd go with it how long he'd ride my tail and scatter after all the sick crumbs dropping from my life till as it seemed to me it became his purpose his reason for being maybe what made him whole useful as sliding outta my skin was my purpose moving on with slick sticky fresh painful to the touch flesh going on pink blood ready to tear down anything anyone in my path make it new make myself new and hurting always hurting so I'd need my friend in syringe to hurt me finally by making me feel calm in its grip carting me to the grave all eyes around his now in especial maybe feeling the slightest tinge of sorrow sorry for me which milked me warmed me made me feel loved.

Moved in with him then always moving anyplace find a place to flop avoid rent or stay ahead of it and move on quick drugs till he latching onto the idea once of brewing it ourselves went in those early days collecting Sudafed in bulk cooking it up wherever we found ourselves as was easy enough done and once we settled down a bit for a stretch put some money in our pockets quickly reinvested in whatever hammerblow drug craze was circling then designer to think ourselves stylish and I cleaned houses watched kids if you can imagine when the money was short for as long as they'd keep me or I'd fuck up or get caught robbing em blind one time unhinged in the toilet with 13-year-old son smoking crack simply sent to the curb outoftheirshock at the instant then inability to track me later or outta some desire not to have their name drug into any involvement with the cops their groomed scholar a crack addict so I skated free and on to the next as was easily enough done fell over the wheel spinning once more into blackness waking next to him my red gray room ecstatic in the orange curls of his sleeping heaving chest.

How we woke sometime in San Francisco I do not know but did in its weaving sleepiness by sea trudged our way up thru lines of gliding roller blade rollicking headphoned fools who'd just come or would be going to ties soon enough polished shoes and briefcase importancy up we'd go and kept till crossing over into Oakland where we settled once again feeling down among our own once again going nowhere expecting nothing but the score the check deliverance.

And we kept to ourselves mostly wandering only for groceries or toilet paper or the like days on end bunkered up in dilapidated hood the blinds drawn shooting what and whatever breathed into us as smoke running juice thru veins bulging ready to scramble free from our skins and flail frantic in stale life room cut just to have it over with but then waking a bit as a bubble expounding from mud to breathe air but still languor and slip back knowing you needed to get free or else but what was there and where and how and was it would it ever be worth it.

So the kick as trying to be sociable frequenting bars he obtaining factory work somehow and actually cleaning up quite a bit that my guilt of my everdeepening slip tugged me back to Catholic pew lodging slipping into wood traps purified air heavy by the smoking it so he'd look at me and laugh as I went unable to reach up to him from the dank mud of my sacrifice but only go deeper deeper gurgling into neath the weight of lounging predecessors dead from the weight of ever dying.

Let's go out he saying then one night let's go out the town somewhere does awaits us and began laughing.

So we went.

Crazy in dread scope weave of near madness.

Went.

Out.

And somehow stumbled.

Thru train station and where bathrooms I think running mad already coursed heavily with the junk went.

To a bar.

A shack really.

And found you.

The writer.

You.

Whom I'd known ages before.

A ghost.

Waiting there for me.

Alone at the bar.

I seized.

And screamed to you locked away in my head.

So that probably only I could hear me.

I screamed.

What will it be?

What do you have in store for me?

This time?

ABOUT THE AUTHOR

MATT MARSHALL writes for *AllAboutJazz.com*. His work has also appeared in *Jazz Inside Magazine*, *Cleveland Scene*, *Cleveland Free Times* and various print and online literary journals. He lives in Cleveland Heights, Ohio.

mattmarshallwriter.com

CPSIA information can be obtained at www.ICGtesting.com
Printed in the USA
LVOW07s1749111115

462081LV00009B/963/P